The shotgun felt heavy in her hands as she started toward the back door.

Dana heard the creak of a footfall on the porch steps. Another creak. The knob on the back door started to turn.

She raised the shotgun.

"Dana?"

The shotgun sagged in her arms as the back door opened and she saw Hud's familiar outline in the doorway.

He froze at the sight of the shotgun.

"I didn't hear you drive up," she whispered.

"I walked the last part of the way so your visitor wouldn't hear me coming and run. When I didn't see any lights on, I circled the house and found the back door unlocked—" His voice broke as he stepped toward her, and she saw how afraid he'd been for her.

He took the shotgun from her and set it aside before cupping her shoulders in his large palms. She could feel his heat even through the thick gloves he wore and smell his scent mixed with the cold night air. It felt so natural, she almost stepped into his arms.

Dear Reader,

We hope you enjoy *Crime Scene at Cardwell Ranch*, written by *USA TODAY* bestselling author B.J. Daniels.

Harlequin Intrigue is the ultimate romantic suspense series. If you love following trace evidence and tracking down leads right along with lawmen and investigators, we have a terrific lineup of six can't-put-down stories available every month.

Join us at Harlequin Intrigue as we crack the hardest cases and unravel the deepest mysteries of the heart.

Happy reading,

The Harlequin Intrigue Editors

P.S. Visit www.tryharlequin.com to download more than 16 free books and experience the variety of romances that we publish!

CRIME SCENE AT CARDWELL RANCH

B.J. DANIELS

TORONTO NEW YORK LONDON
AMSTERDAM PARIS SYDNEY HAMBURG
STOCKHOLM ATHENS TOKYO MILAN MADRID
PRAGUE WARSAW BUDAPEST AUCKLAND

When I think of the Gallatin Canyon, I remember rubber
gun fights at our cabin, hikes to Lava Lake and stopping by
Bessie and Russell Rehm's place near the current Big Sky.
Russell is gone now, but I will always remember Bessie's
cooking—and the treat she used to make me at her ranch
in Texas: a mixture of peanut butter and molasses.
I still make it, and I always think of Bessie.

This book is for you, Bessie.
Thanks for all the memories!

Copyright © 2011 by Harlequin Books S.A.

ISBN-13: 978-0-373-20281-2

The contents of this book may have been
edited from its original format. The publisher
acknowledges the copyright holder of the
individual work as follows:

CRIME SCENE AT CARDWELL RANCH
Copyright © 2006 by Barbara Heinlein

Recycling programs
for this product may
not exist in your area.

www.Harlequin.com

Printed in U.S.A.

ABOUT THE AUTHOR

USA TODAY bestselling author **B.J. Daniels** began writing novels after a career as a newspaper journalist. The author of more than fifty titles for Harlequin Books, she has won numerous awards, including a career achievement award for romantic suspense. Her books regularly appear on bestseller lists.

B.J. lives in Montana with her husband and their two springer spaniels. When she isn't plotting her next book, she snowboards, camps, boats and plays tennis. She is a member of Mystery Writers of America, Sisters in Crime, Thriller Writers, Kiss of Death and Romance Writers of America.

Visit her website at www.bjdaniels.com or email her at bjdaniels@mtintouch.net.

Look for B.J. Daniels's next books from Harlequin Intrigue!

CAST OF CHARACTERS

Dana Cardwell—Her two great loves were her family ranch and Hud Savage. She'd already lost one and now, just when she was about to lose the other, a body was found in the old homestead's well.

Marshal Hud Savage—He was back in town, determined to find out who had set him up to lose not only his former deputy job but also the woman he loved.

Rupert Milligan—The aging coroner thought he'd seen it all—until he climbed down into the old dry well to retrieve the body.

Ginger Adams—Right until the end, she thought that love could conquer all. Unfortunately, she was dead wrong.

Lanny Rankin—The lawyer had always wanted Dana. But how far would he go to have her?

Judge Raymond Randolph—Was the judge's death just a robbery gone wrong, or had the judge become too much of a liability because of what he knew?

Kitty Randolph—The widow had buried herself in charity work to forget her husband's murder five years ago. But the discovery of the body in the well brought it all back.

Jordan Cardwell—He needed money badly if he hoped to keep his lifestyle—and his young, gorgeous, unemployed, former-model wife.

Clay Cardwell—He tried to stay out of the family politics, but if he could get his share of the ranch he could live his secret dream.

Stacy Cardwell—The divorcée had a secret that was eating her alive.

Brick Savage—The former marshal was loved and hated—especially by Judge Raymond Randolph. But his son, Hud, couldn't really believe he was a murderer, could he?

Prologue

Seventeen years earlier

The fall knocked the air out of her. She'd landed badly, one leg bent under her. On the way down, she'd hit her head and the skin on her arms and legs was scraped raw.

Stunned, she tried to get to her feet in the darkness of the tight, confined space. She'd lost both shoes, her body ached and her left hand was in terrible pain, her fingers definitely broken.

She managed to get herself upright in the pitch-blackness of the hole. Bracing herself on the cold earth around her, she looked up, still dazed.

Above her, she could see a pale circle of starlit sky. She started to open her mouth to call out when she heard him stagger to the edge of the old dry well and fall to his knees. His shadow silhouetted over part of the opening.

She stared up at him in confusion. He hadn't meant to push her. He'd just been angry with her. He wouldn't hurt her. Not on purpose.

The beam of a flashlight suddenly blinded her. "Help me."

He made a sound, an eerie, low-keening wail like a wounded animal. "You're alive?"

His words pierced her heart like a cold blade. He'd thought the fall would kill her? *Hoped* it would?

The flashlight went out. She heard him stumble to his feet and knew he was standing looking down at her. She could see his shadow etched against the night sky. She felt dizzy and sick, still too stunned by what had happened.

His shadow disappeared. She could see the circle of dim light above her again. She listened, knowing he hadn't left. He wouldn't leave her. He was just upset, afraid she would tell.

If she pleaded with him the way she had the other times, he would forgive her. He'd tried to break it off before, but he'd always come back to her. He loved her.

She stared up until, with relief, she saw again his dark shape against the starlit sky. He'd gone to get a rope or something to get her out. "I'm sorry. Please, just help me. I won't cause you any more trouble."

"No, you won't." His voice sounded so strange, so foreign. Not the voice of the man she'd fallen so desperately in love with.

She watched him raise his arm. In the glint of starlight she saw it wasn't a rope in his hand.

Her heart caught in her throat. "No!" The gunshot boomed, a deafening roar in the cramped space.

She must have blacked out. When she woke, she was curled in an awkward position in the bottom of the dry well. Over the blinding pain in her head, she could hear the sound of the pickup's engine. He was driving away!

"No!" she cried as she dragged herself up onto her feet again. "Don't leave me here!" As she looked up to the opening high above her, she felt something wet and sticky run down into her eye. Blood.

He'd shot her. The pain in her skull was excruciating. She dropped to her knees on the cold, hard earth. He'd said he loved her. He'd promised to take care of her. Tonight, she'd even worn the red dress he loved.

"Don't leave! Please!" But she knew he couldn't hear her. As she listened, the sound of the engine grew fainter and fainter, then nothing.

She shivered in the damp, cold blackness, her right hand going to her stomach.

He'd come back.

He couldn't just leave her here to die. How could he live with himself if he did?

He'd come back.

Chapter One

As the pickup bounced along the muddy track to
the old homestead, Dana Cardwell stared out at the
wind-scoured Montana landscape, haunted by the
premonition she'd had the night before.

She had awakened in the darkness to the howl
of the unusually warm wind against her bedroom
window and the steady drip of melting snow from
the eaves. A chinook had blown in.

When she'd looked out, she'd seen the bare old
aspens vibrating in the wind, limbs etched black
against the clear night sky. It felt as if something
had awakened her to warn her.

The feeling had been so strong that she'd had trouble getting back to sleep only to wake this morning to
Warren Fitzpatrick banging on the door downstairs.

"There's something you'd better see," the elderly
ranch manager had said.

And now, as Warren drove them up the bumpy
road from the ranch house to the old homestead, she
felt a chill at the thought of what waited for her at
the top of the hill. Was this what she'd been warned
about?

Warren pulled up next to the crumbling foundation and cut the engine. The wind howled across the open hillside, making the tall yellowed grass keel over and gently rocking the pickup.

It was called the January Thaw. Without the blanket of white snow, the land looked wrung out, all color washed from the hills until everything was a dull brown-gray. The only green was a few lone pines swaying against the wind-rinsed sky.

Little remained of the homestead house. Just part of the rock foundation and the fireplace, the chimney as stark as the pines against the horizon.

Past it, in the soft, wet earth, Dana saw Warren's tracks where he had walked to the old well earlier this morning. All that marked the well was a circle of rock and a few weathered boards that covered part of the opening.

Warren cocked his head as if he already heard the marshal's SUV coming up the ranch road. Dana strained her ears but heard nothing over the pounding of her heart.

She was glad Warren had always been a man of few words. She was already on edge without having to talk about what he'd found.

The ranch manager was as dried out as a stick of jerky and just as tough, but he knew more about cattle than any man Dana had ever known. And he was as loyal as an old dog. Until recently, he and Dana had run the ranch together. She knew Warren wouldn't have gotten her up here unless it was serious.

As Dana caught the whine of the approaching vehicle over the wind, the sound growing louder, her dread grew with it.

Warren had told her last night that he'd noticed the boards were off the old dry well again. "I think I'll just fill it in. Safer that way. Give me something to do."

Like a lot of Montana homesteads, the well was just a hole in the ground, unmarked except for maybe a few old boards thrown over it, and because of that, dangerous to anyone who didn't know it was there.

"Whatever you think," she'd told him the night before. She'd been distracted and really hadn't cared.

But she cared now. She just hoped Warren was wrong about what he'd seen in the bottom of the well.

They'd know soon enough, she thought as she turned to watch the Gallatin Canyon marshal's black SUV come roaring up the road from the river.

"Scrappy's driving faster than usual," she said, frowning. "You must have lit a fire under him when you called him this morning."

"Scrappy Morgan isn't marshal anymore," Warren said.

"What?" She glanced over at him. He had a strange look on his weathered face.

"Scrappy just up and quit. They had to hire a temporary marshal to fill in for a while."

"How come I never hear about these things?" But she knew the answer to that. She'd always been too busy on the ranch to keep up with canyon gossip. Even now that she worked down in Big Sky, her ties were still more with the ranching community—what little of it was left in the Gallatin Canyon since the town of Big Sky had sprung up at the base of Lone Mountain. A lot of the ranchers had sold out or sub-divided to take advantage of having a ski and summer resort so close by.

"So who's the interim marshal?" she asked as the Sheriff's Department SUV bounded up the road, the morning sun glinting off the windshield. She groaned. "Not Scrappy's nephew Franklin? Tell me it's anyone but him."

Warren didn't answer as the new marshal brought the black SUV with the Montana State marshal logo on the side to a stop right next to her side of the pickup.

All the breath rushed from her as she looked over and saw the man behind the wheel.

"Maybe I should have warned you," Warren said, sounding sheepish.

"That would've been nice," she muttered be-tween gritted teeth as she met Hudson Savage's clear blue gaze. His look gave nothing away. The two of them might have been strangers—instead of former lovers—for all the expression that showed in his handsome face.

Her emotions boiled up like one of the Yellow-stone geysers just down the road. First shock and right on its heels came fury. When Hud had left town five years ago, she'd convinced herself she'd never have to lay eyes on that sorry son of a bitch again. And here he was. Damn, just when she thought things couldn't get any worse.

OVER THE YEARS as a policeman in L.A., Hudson "Hud" Savage had stared down men who were bigger and stronger. Some had guns, some knives and base-ball bats.

But none unnerved him like the look in Dana Cardwell's whiskey-brown glare.

He dragged his gaze away, turning to pick up the heavy-duty flashlight from the seat next to him. *Coward.* If just seeing her had this effect on him, he hated to think what talking would do.

Her reaction to him was pretty much what he'd expected. He'd known she would be far from happy to see him. But he had hoped she wouldn't be as furious as she'd been when he'd left town. But given the look in her eyes, he'd say that was one wasted hope.

And damn if it was no less painful than it had been five years ago seeing her anger, her hurt.

Not that he blamed her. He hadn't just left town, he'd flat-out run, tail tucked between his legs.

But he was back now.

He picked up the flashlight and, bracing himself against the wind and Dana Cardwell, he opened his door and stepped out.

The sun glinted off the truck's windshield so he couldn't see her face as he walked to the front of the SUV. But he could feel her gaze boring into him like a bullet as he snugged his Stetson down to keep it from sailing off in the wind.

When Warren had called the office this morning, Hud had instructed him not to go near the well again. The ranch foreman's original tracks to and from the well were the only ones in the soft dirt. It surprised

Hud, though, that Dana hadn't gotten out to take a look before he arrived. She obviously hadn't known the order was from him or she would have defied it sure as the devil.

As he looked out across the ranch, memories of the two of them seemed to blow through on the breeze. He could see them galloping on horseback across that far field of wild grasses, her long, dark hair blowing back, face lit by sunlight, eyes bright, grinning at him as they raced back to the barn.

They'd been so young, so in love. He felt that old ache, desire now coupled with heartbreak and regret.

Behind him, he heard first one pickup door open, then the other. The first one closed with a click, the second slammed hard. He didn't have to guess whose door that had been.

Out of the corner of his eye, he saw Warren hang back, waiting by the side of his pickup, out of the way—and out of earshot as well as the line of fire. Warren was no fool.

"Are we goin' to stand here all day admiring the scenery or are we goin' to take a look in the damned well?" Dana asked as she joined Hud.

He let out a bark of nervous laughter and looked over at her, surprised how little she'd changed and glad of it. She was small, five-four compared to his six-six. She couldn't weigh a hundred and ten pounds soaking wet, but what there was of her was a combination of soft curves and hard-edged stubborn determination. To say he'd never known anyone like her was putting it mildly.

He wanted to tell her why he'd come back, but the glint in her eye warned him she was no more ready to hear it than she'd been when he'd left.

"Best take a look in that well then," he said.

"Good idea." She stood back as he trailed Warren's tracks to the hole in the ground.

A half-dozen boards had once covered the well. Now only a couple remained on the single row of rocks rimming the edge. The other boards appeared to have been knocked off by the wind or fallen into the well.

He flipped on the flashlight and shone the beam down into the hole. The well wasn't deep, about fifteen feet, like looking off the roof of a two-story house. Had it been deeper, Warren would never have seen what lay in the bottom.

Hud leaned over the opening, the wind whistling in his ears, the flashlight beam a pale gold as it skimmed the dirt bottom—and the bones.

Hunting with his father as a boy, Hud had seen his share of remains over the years. The sun-bleached skeletons of deer, elk, moose, cattle and coyotes were strewn all over rural Montana.

But just as Warren had feared, the bones lying at the bottom of the Cardwell Ranch dry well weren't from any wild animal.

DANA STOOD BACK, her hands in the pockets of her coat, as she stared at Hud's broad back.

She wished she didn't know him so well. The moment he'd turned on the flashlight and looked down, she'd read the answer in his shoulders. Her already upset stomach did a slow roll and she thought for a moment she might be sick.

Dear God, what was in the well? *Who* was in the well?

Hud glanced back at her, his blue eyes drilling her to the spot where she stood, all the past burning there like a hot blue flame.

But instead of heat, she shivered as if a cold wind blew up from the bottom of the well. A cold that could chill in ways they hadn't yet imagined as Hud straightened and walked back to her.

"Looks like remains of something, all right," Hud said, giving her that same noncommittal look he had when he'd driven up.

The wind whipped her long dark hair around her face. She took a painful breath and let it go, fighting the wind, fighting a weakness in herself that made her angry and scared. "They're human bones, aren't they?"

Hud dragged his hat off and raked a hand through his hair, making her fingers tingle remembering the feel of that thick sun-streaked mop of his. "Won't be certain until we get the bones to the lab."

She looked away, angry at him on so many levels that it made it hard to be civil. "I *know* there are human remains down there. Warren said he saw a human skull. So stop lying to me."

Hud's eyes locked with hers and she saw anger spark in all that blue. He didn't like being called a liar. But then, she could call him much worse if she got started.

"From what I can see, the skull appears to be human. Satisfied?" he said.

She turned away from the only man who had ever satisfied her. She tried not to panic. If having Hud back—let alone the interim marshal—wasn't bad enough, there was a body in the well on her family ranch. She tried to assure herself that the bones could have been in the well for years. The well had been dug more than a hundred years ago. Who knew how long the bones had been there?

But the big question, the same one she knew Hud had to be asking, was *why* the bones were there.

"I'm going to need to cordon this area off," he said. "I would imagine with it being calving season, you have some cattle moving through here?"

"No cattle in here to worry about," Warren said.

Hud frowned and glanced out across the ranch. "I didn't notice any cattle on the way in, either."

Dana felt his gaze shift to her. She pulled a hand from her pocket to brush a strand of her hair from her face before looking at him. The words stuck in her throat and she was grateful to Warren when he said, "The cattle were all auctioned this fall to get the ranch ready to sell."

Hud looked stunned, his gaze never leaving hers. "You wouldn't sell the ranch."

She turned her face away from him. He was the one person who knew just what this ranch meant to her and yet she didn't want him to see that selling it was breaking her heart just as he had. She could feel his gaze on her as if waiting for her to explain.

When she didn't, he said, "I have to warn you, Dana, this investigation might hold up a sale."

She hadn't thought of that. She hadn't thought of anything but the bones—and her added bad luck in finding out that Hud was acting marshal.

"Word is going to get out, if it hasn't already," he continued. "Once we get the bones up, we'll know more, but this investigation could take some time."

"You do whatever you have to do, Hud." She hadn't said his name out loud in years. It sounded odd and felt even stranger on her tongue. Amazing that such a small word could hurt so much.

She turned and walked back to Warren's pickup, surprised her legs held her up. Her mind was reeling. There was a body in a well on her ranch? And Hud Savage was back after all this time of believing him long gone? She wasn't sure which shocked or terrified her more.

She didn't hear him behind her until he spoke.

"I was sorry to hear about your mother," he said so close she felt his warm breath on her neck and caught a whiff of his aftershave. The same kind he'd used when he was hers.

Without turning, she gave a nod of her head, the wind burning her eyes, and jerked open the pickup door, sending a glance to Warren across the hood that she was more than ready to leave.

As she climbed into the truck and started to pull the door shut behind her, Hud dropped one large palm over the top of the door to keep it from closing. "Dana…"

She shot him a look she thought he might still remember, the same one a rattler gives right before it strikes.

"I just wanted to say...happy birthday."

She tried not to show her surprise—or her pleasure—that he'd remembered. That he had, though, made it all the worse. She swallowed and looked up at him, knifed with that old familiar pain, the kind that just never went away no matter how hard you fought it.

"Dana, listen—"

"I'm engaged." The lie was out before she could call it back.

Hud's eyebrows rose. "To anyone I know?"

She took guilty pleasure from the pain she heard in his voice, saw in his face. "Lanny Rankin."

"Lanny? The *lawyer?*" Hud didn't sound surprised, just contemptuous. He must have heard that she'd been dating Lanny. "He still saving up for the ring?"

"What?"

"An engagement ring. You're not wearing one." He motioned to her ring finger.

Silently she swore at her own stupidity. She'd wanted to hurt him and at the same time keep him at a safe distance. Unfortunately she hadn't given a thought to the consequences.

"I just forgot to put it on this morning," she said.

"Oh, you take it off at night?"

Another mistake. When Hud had put the engagement ring on her finger so many years ago now, she'd sworn she'd never take it off.

"If you must know," she said, "the diamond got caught in my glove, so I took it off to free it and must have laid it down."

His brows went up again.

Why didn't she just shut up? "I was in a hurry this morning. Not that it's any of your business."

"You're right," he agreed. "Must be a big diamond to get stuck in a glove." Not like the small chip he'd been able to afford for her, his tone said.

"Look, as far as I'm concerned, you and I have nothing to say to each other."

"Sorry, didn't mean to pry into your personal life." A muscle bunched in his jaw and he took on that all-business marshal look again. "I'd appreciate it if you and Warren wouldn't mention what you found in the well to anyone. I know it's going to get out, but I'd like to try to keep a lid on it as long as we can."

He had to be joking. The marshal's office dispatcher was the worst gossip in the canyon.

"Anything else?" she asked pointedly as his hand remained on the door.

His gaze softened again and she felt her heart do that pitter-patter thing it hadn't done since Hud.

"It's good seeing you again, Dana," he said.

"I wish I could say the same, Hud."

His lips turned up in a rueful smile as she jerked hard on the door, forcing him to relinquish his hold. If only she could free herself as easily.

The pickup door slammed hard. Warren got in and started the engine without a word. She knew he'd heard her lie about being engaged, but Warren was too smart to call her on it.

As sun streamed into the cab, Warren swung the pickup around. Dana rolled down her window, flushed with a heat that had nothing to do with the warmth of the sun or the January Thaw. She could see the ranch house down the hillside. Feel the rattle of the tires over the rough road, hear the wind in the pines.

She promised herself she wouldn't do it even as she reached out, her fingers trembling, and adjusted the side mirror to look back.

Hud was still standing where she'd left him, looking after them.

Happy birthday.

Chapter Two

Well, that had gone better than he'd expected, Hud thought with his usual self-deprecating sarcasm.

She was *engaged* to Lanny Rankin?

What did you expect? It's been years. I'm surprised she isn't married by now. But Lanny Rankin?

He watched the pickup disappear over the hill, listening until the sound of the engine died away and all he could hear was the wind again.

Yeah, why *isn't* she married?

Lanny Rankin had gone after Dana before Hud had even driven out past the city limit sign. He'd had five years. So why weren't the two of them married?

He felt a glimmer of hope.

Was it possible Dana was dragging her feet because she was still in love with him—not Lanny Rankin?

And why wasn't she wearing her ring? Maybe she didn't even have one. Maybe she wasn't engaged—at least not officially.

Maybe you're clutching at straws.

Maybe, but his instincts told him that if she was going to marry Lanny, she would have by now.

A half mile down the hillside, he could see Warren's pickup stop in a cloud of dust. Hud watched Dana get out. She was still beautiful. Still prickly as a porcupine. Still strong and determined. Still wishing him dead.

He couldn't blame her for that, though.

He had a terrible thought. What if she married Lanny now just out of spite?

And what was this about selling the ranch? The old Dana Cardwell he knew would never put the ranch up for sale. Was she thinking about leaving after it sold? Worse, after she married Lanny?

She disappeared into the ranch house. This place was her heart. She'd always said she would die here and be buried up on the hill with the rest of her mother's family, the Justices.

He'd loved that about her, her pride in her family's past, her determination to give that lifestyle to her children—to *their* children.

Hud felt that gut-deep ache of regret. God, how he hated what he'd done to her. What he'd done to himself. It didn't help that he'd spent the past five years trying to make sense of it.

Water under the bridge, his old man would have said. But then his old man didn't have a conscience. Made life easier that way, Hud thought, cursing at even the thought of Brick Savage. He thought of all the wasted years he'd spent trying to please his father—and the equally wasted years he'd spent hating him.

Hud turned, disgusted with himself, and tried to lose himself in the one thing that gave him any peace, his work.

He put in a call to Coroner Rupert Milligan. While he waited for Rupert, he shot both digital photographs and video of the site, trying not to speculate on the bones in the well or how they had gotten there.

Rupert drove up not thirty minutes later. He was dressed in a suit and tie, which in Montana meant either a funeral or a wedding. "Toastmasters, if you have to know," he said as he walked past Hud to the well, grabbing the flashlight from Hud's hand on his way.

Rupert Milligan was older than God and more powerful in this county. Tall, white-haired, with a head like a buffalo, he had a gruff voice and little patience for stupidity. He'd retired as a country doctor but still worked as coroner. He'd gotten hooked on murder mysteries—and forensics. Rupert loved nothing better than a good case and while Hud was still hoping the bones weren't human, he knew that Rupert was pitching for the other team.

Rupert shone the flashlight down into the well, leaning one way then the other. He froze, holding the flashlight still as he leaned down even farther. Hud figured he'd seen the skull partially exposed at one edge of the well.

"You got yourself a human body down there, but then I reckon you already knew that," he said, sounding too cheerful as he straightened.

Hud nodded.

"Let's get it out of there." Rupert had already started toward his rig.

Hud would have offered to go down in Rupert's place but he knew the elderly coroner wouldn't have stood for it. All he needed Hud for was to document it if the case ever went to trial—and help winch him and the bones out of the well.

He followed Rupert over to his pickup where the coroner had taken off his suit jacket and was pulling on a pair of overalls.

"Wanna put some money on what we got down there?" Rupert asked with a grin. Among his other eclectic traits, Rupert was a gambler. To his credit, he seldom lost.

"Those bones could have been down there for fifty years or more," Hud said, knowing that if that was the case, there was a really good chance they would never know the identity of the person or how he'd ended up down there.

Rupert shook his head as he walked around to the back of the truck and dropped the tailgate. "Those aren't fifty-year-old bones down there. Not even close."

The coroner had come prepared. There was a pulley system in the back and a large plastic box with a body bag, latex gloves, a variety of different size containers, a video camera and a small shovel.

He handed Hud the pulley then stuffed the needed items into a backpack, which he slung over his shoulder before slipping a headlamp over his white hair and snapping it on.

"True, it's dry down there, probably been covered most of the time since the bones haven't been bleached by the sun," Rupert said as he walked back to the well and Hud followed. "Sides of the well are too steep for most carnivores. Insects would have been working on the bones, though. Maggots." He took another look into the well. "Spot me five years and I'll bet you fifty bucks that those bones have been down there two decades or less," he said with his usual confidence, a confidence based on years of experience.

Twenty years ago Hud would have been thirteen. Rupert would have been maybe forty-five. With a jolt Hud realized that Rupert wasn't that much older than his father. It felt odd to think of Brick Savage as old. In Hud's mind's eye he saw his father at his prime, a large, broad-shouldered man who could have been an actor. Or even a model. He was that good-looking.

"I got a hundred that says whoever's down there didn't fall down there by accident," Rupert said.

"Good thing I'm not a betting man," Hud said, distracted. His mind on the fact that twenty years ago, his father was marshal.

"TELL ME you didn't," Dana said as she walked into Needles and Pins and heard giggling in the back beyond the racks of fabric.

Her best friend and partner in the small sewing shop gave her a grin and a hug. "It's your birthday, kiddo," Hilde whispered. "Gotta celebrate."

"Birthdays after thirty should not be celebrated," Dana whispered back.

"Are you kidding? And miss seeing what thirty-one candles on a cake looks like?"

"You didn't."

Hilde had her arm and was tugging her toward the back. "Smile. I promise this won't kill you, though you do look like you think it will." She slowed. "You're shaking. Seriously, are you all right?"

As much as she hated it, Dana was still a wreck after seeing Hud again. She'd hoped to get to work at the shop and forget about everything that had happened this morning, including not only what might be in the old well—but also who. The last thing she wanted was to even be reminded of her birthday. It only reminded her that Hud had remembered.

"Hud's back," she said, the words coming out in a rush.

Hilde stopped dead so that Dana almost collided with her.

Her best friend's surprise made her feel better. Dana had been worried all morning that everyone had known about Hud's return—and just hadn't told her to protect her. She hated being protected. Especially from news like that. If she'd known he was back, she could have prepared herself for seeing him— Even as she thought it, she knew nothing could have prepared her for that initial shock of seeing Hud after five long years.

"Hud's back in the canyon?" Hilde whispered, sounding shocked. The Gallatin Canyon, a fifty-mile strip of winding highway and blue-ribbon river, had been mostly ranches, the cattle and dude kind, a few summer cabins and homes—that is until Big Sky resort and the small town that followed at the foot of Lone Mountain. But the "canyon" was still its own little community.

"Hud's the new temporary marshal," Dana whispered, her throat suddenly dry.

"Hello?" came the familiar voice of Margo from the back of the store. "We've got candles burning up in here."

"Hud? Back here? Oh, man, what a birthday present," Hilde said, giving her another hug. "I'm so sorry, sweetie. I can imagine what seeing him again did to you."

"I still want to kill him," Dana whispered.

"Not on your birthday." Hilde frowned. "Does Lanny know yet?" she whispered.

"Lanny? Lanny and I are just friends."

"Does Lanny know that?" her friend asked, giving her a sympathetic smile.

"He knows." Dana sighed, remembering the night Lanny had asked her to marry him and she'd had to turn him down. Things hadn't been the same between them since. "I did something really stupid. I told Hud I was engaged to Lanny."

"You didn't."

Dana nodded miserably. "I don't know what I was thinking."

Margo called from the back room. "Major wax guttering back here."

"Let's get this over with," Dana said, and she and Hilde stepped into the back of the shop where a dozen of Dana's friends and store patrons had gathered around a cake that looked like it was on fire.

"Quick! Make a wish!" her friend Margo cried.

Dana closed her eyes for an instant, made a wish, then braving the heat of thirty-one candles flickering on a sheet cake, blew as hard as she could, snuffing out every last one of them to the second chorus of "Happy Birthday."

"Tell me you didn't wish Hud dead," Hilde whispered next to her as the smoke started to dissipate.

"And have my wish not come true? No way."

HUD WATCHED RUPERT, the glow of the coroner's headlamp flickering eerily on the dark dirt walls as he descended into the well. Hud tried not to think about remains down there or the fact that Brick might have investigated the disappearance. Might even have known the victim. Just as Hud and Rupert might have.

Rupert stopped the pulley just feet above the bones to video the scene on the bottom of the well. The light flickered and Hud looked away as he tried to corral his thoughts. Sure as hell this investigation would force him to deal with his father. The thought turned his stomach. The last time he'd seen his father, more than five years ago now, they'd almost ended up in a brawl, burning every bridge between them—both content with the understanding that the next time Hud saw his father it would be to make sure Brick was buried.

When Hud had decided to come back, he'd thought at least he wouldn't have to see his father. Word was that Brick had moved to a place up on Hebgen Lake near West Yellowstone—a good fifty miles away.

The wind seemed cooler now and in the distance Hud could see dark clouds rolling up over the mountains. He turned his face up to the pale sun knowing it wouldn't be long before it was snowing again. After all, this was January in Montana.

The rope on the pulley groaned and he looked down again into the well as Rupert settled gently on the bottom, the headlamp now focused on the human remains.

Because of the steep sides of the well, the body was contained, none of the bones had been scattered by critters or carried off. The coroner had pulled on a pair of the latex gloves. He opened the body bag and began to carefully fill it with the bones.

"Good thing you didn't bet with me," Rupert said. "I'd say the bones have been here closer to fifteen years." He held up a pelvic bone in his gloved hands. "A woman. White. Late twenties, early thirties."

In the light from the headlamp, Hud watched Rupert pick up the skull and turn it slowly in his hands.

"Well, how about that," he heard Rupert say, then glance up at him. "You got a murder on your hands, son," the coroner said solemnly. He held up the skull, his headlamp shining through a small round hole in it.

"The bullet entered this side, passed through the brain and lodged in the mastoid bone behind the left ear," Rupert said, still turning the skull in his hands. "The bullet lead is flattened and deformed from impact but there will be enough lands and grooves to match the weapon. Looks like a .38."

"If we could find the weapon after all this time," Hud said. He let out an oath under his breath. Murder. And the body found on the Cardwell Ranch.

"Get one of those containers out of my rig so I can bag the skull separately," Rupert said, his voice echoing up.

Hud ran back to Rupert's truck and returned to lower the container down to him. A few minutes later Rupert sent the filled container up and Hud found himself looking at the dead woman's skull. A patch of hair clung to the top. The hair, although covered with dirt, was still reddish in color. He stared at the hair, at the shape of the skull, and tried to picture the face.

"You think she was young, huh?" he called down.

In the well, Rupert stopped to inspect one of the bones in the light from his headlamp. "Based on growth lines, I'd say twenty-eight to thirty-five years of age." He put down one bone to pick up what appeared to be a leg bone. "Hmm, that's interesting. The bony prominences show muscle development, indicating she spent a lot of time on her feet. Probably made her living as a hairdresser, grocery clerk, nurse, waitress, something like that." He put the bone into the body bag and picked up another shorter one. "Same bony prominences on the arms as if she often carried something heavy. My money's on waitress or nurse."

Few coroners would go out on a limb with such conjecture. Most left this part up to the forensics team at the state crime lab. But then, Rupert Milligan wasn't like most coroners. Add to that the fact that he was seldom wrong.

"What about height and weight?" Hud asked, feeling a chill even in the sun. His father had always liked waitresses. Hell, his father chased skirts no matter who wore them.

Rupert seemed to study the dirt where the bones had been. "I'd say she was between five-four and five-seven. A hundred and twenty to a hundred and forty pounds."

That covered a lot of women, Hud thought as he carried the container with the skull in it over to Rupert's pickup and placed it carefully on the front seat. All the teeth were still intact. With luck, they'd be able to identify her from dental records if she'd been local.

He tried to remember if he'd heard his father talking about a missing person's case about fifteen years ago. Rodrick "Brick" Savage loved to brag about his cases—especially the ones he solved.

But then this one wouldn't have been one he'd solved. And fifteen years ago, Hud had been eighteen and away at college. He wondered if Dana had mentioned a missing woman in one of her letters to him. She'd written him every week, but the letters were more about what was happening on the ranch, I-miss-you letters, love letters.

Leaving the skull at the pickup, he went back to watch Rupert dig through the dirt on the well floor. The coroner slowed as he hit something, then stooped and shook dirt from what he'd found.

Hud felt his chest heave as Rupert held up a bright red high-heeled shoe.

AFTER THE BIRTHDAY party and in between customers, Dana defied Hud's orders and told Hilde about what Warren had found in the old dry well by the original homestead's foundation.

Dana was sure the news was all over the canyon by now. But still she'd waited, not wanting to say anything to anyone but Hilde, her best friend.

"He really thinks the bones are human?" Hilde asked with a shiver. "Who could it be?"

Dana shook her head. "Probably some ancestor of mine."

Hilde looked skeptical. "You think the bones have been down there that long?" She hugged herself as if she could feel the cold coming up from the well just as Dana had earlier.

"It's horrible to think that someone might have fallen in and been unable to get out, died down there," Dana said.

Hilde nodded. "It's just odd that you found them now." Her eyes lit. "You think the investigation will hold up the sale of the ranch?"

"Maybe, but ultimately the ranch will be sold, trust me," Dana said, and changed the subject. "Thank you for the birthday party. I love the purse you made me."

"You're welcome. I'm sorry you've had such a lousy day. Why don't you go on home? I can handle things here. It's your birthday."

Dana groaned. "I hate to imagine what other horrible things could happen before this day is over."

"Always the optimist, aren't you."

Dana smiled in spite of herself. "I think I will go home." She looked outside. Clouds scudded across the pale sky, taking the earlier warmth with them. The sign over the door pendulumed in the wind and she could almost feel the cold trying to get in.

Across the way from the shop, the top of the mountain had disappeared, shrouded in white clouds. The first snowflakes, blown by the wind, swept across the window. Apparently the weatherman had been right when he'd called for snow before midnight.

Dana would be lucky to get home before the roads iced over.

FROM DOWN IN THE WELL, Rupert signaled for Hud to pull up the body bag. It was heavy, but mostly from the layer of dirt retrieved from the bottom of the well. The dirt would be sifted for evidence later at the state crime lab.

He put down the body bag, noting that the weather had turned. Snowflakes danced around him, pelting him on gusts of wind and momentarily blinding him. He barely felt the cold as he squatted near the edge of the well, pulling up the hood on his marshal's jacket as he watched Rupert finish.

The red high-heeled shoe had triggered something. Not a real memory since he couldn't recall when, where or if he'd even actually seen a woman in a red dress and bright red high-heeled shoes. It could have been a photograph. Even a television show or a movie.

But for just an instant he'd had a flash of a woman in a bright red dress and shoes. She was spinning around in a circle, laughing, her long red hair whirling around her head, her face hidden from view.

That split-second image had left him shaken. Had he known this woman?

The canyon was like a small town except for a few months when the out-of-staters spent time in their vacation homes or condos to take advantage of the skiing or the mild summer weather.

But if the woman had been one of those, Hud knew he'd have heard about her disappearance. More than likely she was someone who'd worked at the resort or one of the local businesses. She might not have even been missed as seasonal workers were pretty transient.

"I'm going to need another container from the truck," Rupert called up.

The wind had a bite to it now. Snowflakes swirled around him as Hud lowered the container down and watched the coroner place what appeared to be a dirt-caked piece of once-red fabric inside. Just as in his memory, the woman had worn a red dress. Rupert continued to sift through the dirt, stooped over in the small area, intent on his work.

Hud pulled his coat around him. The mountains across the canyon were no longer visible through the falling snow. And to think he'd actually missed winters while working for the police department in Los Angeles.

From down in the well, Rupert let out a curse, calling Hud's attention back to the dark hole in the ground.

"What is it?" Hud called down.

Rupert had the video camera out and seemed to be trying to steady his hands as he photographed the well wall.

"You aren't going to believe this." The older man's voice sounded strained as if he'd just found something that had shaken him—a man who'd bragged that he'd seen the worst of everything. "She was still alive."

"What?" Hud asked, his blood running cold.

"Neither the gunshot wound nor being thrown down the well killed her right away," Rupert said. "There are deep gouges in the earth where she tried to climb out."

Chapter Three

Long after Rupert came up out of the well, neither he nor Hud said anything. Snow whirled on the wind, the bank of clouds dropping over them, the sun only a memory.

Hud sat behind the wheel of the SUV, motor running, heater cranked up, drinking coffee from the thermos Rupert had brought. Next to him, Rupert turned the SUV's heater vent so it blew into his face.

The older man looked pale, his eyes hollow. Hud imagined that, like him, Rupert had been picturing what it must have been like being left in the bottom of that well to die a slow death.

The yellow crime scene tape Hud had strung up now bowed in the wind and snow. The hillside was a blur of white, the snow falling diagonally.

"I suppose the murder weapon could still be up here," Hud said to Rupert, more to break the silence than anything else. Even with the wind and the motor and heater going, the day felt too quiet, the hillside too desolate. Anything was better than thinking about the woman in the well—even remembering Dana's reaction to seeing him again.

"Doubt you'll ever find that gun," Rupert said without looking at him. The old coroner had been unusually quiet since coming up out of the well.

Hud had called the sheriff's department in Bozeman and asked for help searching the area. It was procedure, but Hud agreed with Rupert. He doubted the weapon would ever turn up.

Except they had to search for it. Unfortunately this was Montana. A lot of men drove trucks with at least one firearm hanging on the back window gun rack and another in the glove box or under the seat.

"So did he shoot her before or after she went into the well?" Hud asked.

"After, based on the angle the bullet entered her skull." Rupert took a sip of his coffee.

"He must have thought he killed her."

Rupert said nothing as he stared in the direction of the well.

"Had to have known about the well," Hud said. Which meant he had knowledge of the Cardwell Ranch. Hud groaned to himself as he saw where he was headed with this. The old homestead was a good mile off Highway 191 that ran through the Gallatin Canyon. The killer could have accessed the old homestead by two ways. One was the Cardwells' private bridge, which would mean driving right by the ranch house.

Or…he could have taken the Piney Creek Bridge, following a twisted route of old logging roads. The same way he and Dana used when he was late getting her home.

Either way, the killer had to be local to know about the well, let alone the back way. Unless, of course, the killer was a member of the Cardwell family and had just driven in past the ranch house bold as brass.

Why bring the woman here, though? Why the Cardwell Ranch well?

"You know what bothers me?" Hud said, taking a sip of his coffee. "The red high heel. Just one in the well. What happened to the other one? And what was she doing up here dressed like that?" He couldn't shake that flash of memory of a woman in a red dress any more than he could nail down its source.

He felt his stomach tighten when Rupert didn't jump in. It wasn't like Rupert. Did his silence have something to do with realizing the woman in the well hadn't been dead and tried to save herself? Or was it possible Rupert suspected who she was and for some reason was keeping it to himself?

"The heels, the dress, it's almost like she was on a date," Hud said. "Or out for a special occasion."

Rupert glanced over at him. "You might make as good a marshal as your father some day." High praise to Rupert's way of thinking, so Hud tried hard not to take offense.

"Odd place to bring your date, though," Hud commented. But then maybe not. The spot was isolated. Not like a trailhead where anyone could come along. No one would be on this section of the ranch at night and you could see the ranch house and part of the road up the hillside. You would know if anyone was headed in your direction in plenty of time to get away.

And yet it wasn't close enough that anyone could hear a woman's cries for help.

"Still, someone had to have reported her missing," Hud persisted. "A roommate. A boss. A friend. A husband."

Rupert finished his coffee and started to screw the cup back on the thermos. "Want any more?"

Hud shook his head. "You worked with my father for a lot of years."

Rupert looked over at him, eyes narrowing. "Brick Savage was the best damned marshal I've ever known." He said it as if he knew only too well that there were others who would have argued that, Hud among them, and Rupert wasn't going to have it.

Brick Savage was a lot of things. A colorful marshal, loved and respected by supporters, feared and detested by his adversaries. Hud knew him as a stubborn, rigid father who he'd feared as a boy and despised as a man. Hud hated to think of the years he'd tried to prove himself to his father—only to fail.

He could feel Rupert's gaze on him, daring him to say anything against Brick. "If you're right about how long she's been down there…"

Rupert made a rude sound under his breath, making it clear he was right.

"…then Brick would have been marshal and you would have been assistant coroner."

"Your point?" Rupert asked.

Hud eyed him, wondering why Rupert was getting his back up. Because Hud had brought up Brick? "I just thought you might remember a missing person's case during that time."

"You'd have to ask your father. Since no body was found, I might not even have heard about it." Rupert zipped up his coroner jacket he'd pulled from behind the seat of his truck. "I need to get to the crime lab."

Hud handed Rupert the coffee cup he'd lent him. "Just seems odd, doesn't it? Someone had to have missed her. You would think the whole area would have been talking about it."

The coroner smiled ruefully. "Some women come and go more often than a Greyhound bus."

Hud remembered hearing that Rupert's first wife had run off on numerous occasions before she'd finally cleared out with a long-haul truck driver.

"You think this woman was like that?" Hud asked, his suspicion growing that Rupert knew more than he was saying.

"If she was, then your suspect list could be as long as your arm." Rupert opened his door.

"You almost sound as if you have an idea who she was," Hud said over the wind.

Rupert climbed out of the truck. "I'll call you when I know something definite."

Hud watched the older man move through the falling snow and wondered why Rupert, who was ready to bet on the bones earlier, seemed to be backpedaling now. It wasn't like the old coroner. Unless Rupert suspected who the bones belonged to—and it hit a little too close to home.

THE PHONE was ringing as Dana walked through the ranch house door. She dropped the stack of mail she'd picked up at the large metal box down by the highway and rushed to answer the phone, not bothering to check caller ID, something she regretted the moment she heard her older brother's voice.

"Dana, what the hell's going on?" Jordan demanded without even a hello let alone a "happy birthday." Clearly he had been calling for some time, not thinking to try her at her new job.

"Where are you?"

"Where do you think I am?" he shot back. "In case you forgot, I live in New York. What the hell is going on out there?"

She slumped into a chair, weak with relief. For a moment she'd thought he was in Montana, that he'd somehow heard about the bones in the well and had caught a flight out. The last thing she needed today was her brother Jordan to deal with in the flesh. Unfortunately it seemed she would have to deal with him on the phone, though.

Her relief was quickly replaced by irritation with him. "I'm fine, Jordan. Thanks for asking, considering it's my birthday and it's been a rough day." She'd seen the sheriff's department cars go up the road toward the old homestead, making her even more aware of what was happening not a mile from the ranch house.

Jordan let out a weary sigh. "Dana, if this is about the ranch—"

"Jordan, let's not. Not today. Is there a reason you called?"

"Hell yes! I want to know why the marshal thinks there's a body in a well on our ranch."

Our ranch? She gritted her teeth. Jordan had hated everything about the ranch and ranching, distancing himself as far as he could from both.

How had he heard about the bones already? She sighed, thinking of Franklin Morgan's sister, Shirley, who worked as dispatcher. Shirley had dated Jordan in high school and still drooled over him whenever Jordan returned to the canyon. Well, at least Dana didn't have to wonder anymore how long it would take for the word to get out.

She didn't dare tell him that it had been Warren who'd found the bones. Jordan would never understand why Warren hadn't just filled in the well and kept his mouth shut. "I found some bones in the old dry well at the homestead."

"So?"

"I called the marshal's office to report them."

"For God's sake, why?"

"Because it's both legally and morally the thing to do." She really wasn't in the mood for Jordan today.

"This is going to hold up the sale of the ranch."

"Jordan, some poor soul is in the bottom of our well. Whoever it is deserves to be buried properly."

"It's probably just animal bones. I'm flying out there to see what the hell is really going on."

"No!" The word was out before she could call it back. Telling Jordan no was like waving a red blanket in front of a rodeo bull.

"You're up to something. This is just another ploy on your part."

She closed her eyes and groaned inwardly. "I just think it would be better if you didn't come out. I can handle this. You'll only make matters worse."

"I have another call coming in. I'll call you back." He hung up.

Dana gritted her teeth as she put down the phone and picked up her mail and began sorting through it. All she needed was Jordan coming out here now. She thought about leaving so she didn't have to talk to him when he called back.

Or she could just not answer the phone. But she knew that wouldn't accomplish anything other than making him more angry. And Jordan wasn't someone you wanted to deal with when he was angry.

She opened a letter from Kitty Randolph asking her to help chair another fundraiser. Kitty and Dana's mother had been friends and since Mary's death, Kitty had seemed to think that Dana would take her mother's place. Dana put the letter aside. She knew she would probably call Kitty in a day or so and agree to do it. She always did.

She picked up the rest of the mail and froze at the sight of the pale yellow envelope. No return address, but she knew who it was from the moment she saw the handwriting.

Throw it away. Don't even open it.

The last thing she needed was to get something from her sister, Stacy, today.

The envelope was card-shaped. Probably just a birthday card. But considering that she and Stacy hadn't spoken to each other in five years...

She started to toss the envelope in the trash but stopped. Why would her sister decide to contact her now? Certainly not because it was her birthday. No, Stacy was trying to butter her up. Kind of like good cop, bad cop with Jordan opting of course for the bad cop role. Her other brother Clay was more of the duck-for-cover type when there was conflict in the family.

Dana couldn't help herself. She ripped open the envelope, not surprised to find she'd been right. A birthday card.

On the front was a garden full of flowers and the words, *For My Sister*. Dana opened the card.

"Wishing you happiness on your birthday and always."

"Right. Your big concern has always been my happiness," Dana muttered.

The card was signed, Stacy. Then in small print under it were the words, *I am so sorry.*

Dana balled up the card and hurled it across the room, remembering a time when she'd idolized her older sister. Stacy was everything Dana had once wanted to be. Beautiful, popular, the perfect older sister to emulate. She'd envied the way Stacy made everything look easy. On the other hand, Dana had been a tomboy, scuffed knees, unruly hair and not a clue when it came to boys.

What Dana hadn't realized once she grew up was how much Stacy had envied *her*. Or what lengths she would go to to hurt her.

The phone rang. She let it ring twice more before she forced herself to pick up the receiver, not bothering to check caller ID for the second time. "Yes?"

"Dana?"

"Lanny. I thought it…was someone else," she said lamely.

"Is everything all right?" he asked.

She could picture him sitting in his office in his three-piece, pin-striped suit, leaning back in his leather chair, with that slight frown he got when he was in lawyer mode.

"Fine. Just…busy." She rolled her eyes at how stupid she sounded. But she could feel what wasn't being said between them like a speech barrier. Lanny had to have heard that Hud was back in town. Wasn't that why he'd called?

"Well, then I won't keep you. I just wanted to make sure we were still on for tonight," he said.

"Of course." She'd completely forgotten about their date. The last thing she wanted to do was to go out tonight. But she'd made this birthday dinner date weeks ago.

"Great, then I'll see you at eight." He seemed to hesitate, as if waiting for her to say something, then hung up.

Why hadn't she told him the truth? That she was exhausted, that there was a dead body in her well, that she just wanted to stay home and lick her wounds? Lanny would have understood.

But she knew why she hadn't. Because Lanny would think her canceling their date had something to do with Hud.

ONCE THE TEAM OF DEPUTIES on loan from the sheriff's department in Bozeman arrived and began searching the old homestead, Hud drove back to his office at Big Sky.

Big Sky didn't really resemble a town. Condos had sprung up after construction on the famous resort began on the West Fork of the Gallatin River in the early 1970s. A few businesses had followed, along with other resort amenities such as a golf course in the lower meadow and ski area on the spectacular Lone Mountain peak.

The marshal's office was in the lower meadow in a nondescript small wooden building, manned with a marshal, two deputies and a dispatcher. After hours, all calls were routed to the sheriff's office in Bozeman.

Hud had inherited two green deputies and a dispatcher who was the cousin of the former sheriff and the worst gossip in the state. Not much to work with, especially now that he had a murder on his hands.

He parked in the back and entered the rear door, so lost in thought that he didn't hear them at first. He stopped just inside the door at the sound of his name being brandished about.

"Well, you know darned well that he had some kind of pull to get this job, even temporarily." Hud recognized Franklin Morgan's voice. Franklin was the nephew of former marshal Scott "Scrappy" Morgan. Franklin was a sheriff's deputy in Bozeman, some forty miles away.

Hud had been warned that Franklin wasn't happy about not getting the interim marshal job after his uncle left and that there might be some hard feelings. Hud smiled at that understatement as he heard Franklin continue.

"At first I thought he must have bought the job, but hell, the Savages haven't ever had any money." This from Shirley Morgan, the dispatcher, and Franklin's sister. Nepotism was alive and well in the canyon.

"Didn't his mother's family have money?" Franklin asked.

"Well, if they did, they didn't leave it to their daughter after she married Brick Savage," Shirley said. "But then, can you blame them?"

"Hud seems like he knows what he's doing," countered Deputy Norm Turner. Norm was a tall, skinny, shy kid with little to no experience at life or law enforcement from what Hud could tell.

"Maybe Brick pulled some strings to get Hud the job," Franklin said.

Hud scoffed. Brick wouldn't pull on the end of a rope if his son was hanging off it from a cliff on the other end.

"Not a chance," Shirley said with a scornful laugh. "It was that damned Dana Cardwell."

Hud felt a jolt. Dana?

"Everyone in the canyon does what she wants just like they did when her mother was alive. Hell, those Cardwell women have been running things in this canyon for years. Them and Kitty Randolph. You can bet Dana Cardwell got him the job."

Hud couldn't help but smile just thinking how Dana would love to hear that she was responsible for getting him back to town.

Franklin took a drink of his coffee and happened to look up and see Hud standing just inside the doorway. The deputy's eyes went wide, coffee spewing from his mouth. Hud could see the wheels turning. Franklin was wondering how long Hud had been there and just what he'd overheard.

Norm swung around and about choked on the doughnut he'd just shoved into his mouth.

Shirley, who'd been caught before, didn't even bother to look innocent. She just scooted her chair through the open doorway to the room that housed the switchboard, closing the door behind her.

Hud watched with no small amount of amusement as the two deputies tried to regain their composure. "Any word from the crime lab?" Hud asked as he proceeded to his office.

Both men answered at the same time.

"Haven't heard a word."

"Nothing from our end." Franklin tossed his foam coffee cup in the trash as if he suddenly remembered something urgent he needed to do. He hightailed it out of the office.

Deputy Turner didn't have that luxury. "Marshal, about what was being said..."

Hud could have bailed him out, could have pretended he hadn't heard a word, but he didn't. He'd been young once himself. He liked to think he'd learned from his mistakes, but coming back here might prove him wrong.

"It's just that I—I...wanted to say..." The young deputy looked as if he might break down.

"Deputy Turner, don't you think I know that everyone in the canyon is wondering how I got this job, even temporarily, after what happened five years ago? I'm as surprised as anyone that I'm the marshal for the time being. All I can do is prove that I deserve it. How about you?"

"Yes, sir, that's exactly how I feel," he said, his face turning scarlet.

"That's what I thought," Hud said, and continued on to his office.

He was anxious to go through the missing person's file from around fifteen years back. But he quickly saw that all but the past ten years of files had been moved to the Bozeman office.

"We don't have any records back that far," the clerk told him when he called. "We had a fire. All the records were destroyed."

Twelve years ago. He'd completely forgotten about the fire. He hung up. All he could hope was that Rupert was wrong. That the woman hadn't been in the well more than twelve years. Otherwise... He swore.

Otherwise, he would be forced to talk to the former marshal. After all this time, the last thing Hud wanted was to see his father.

"I'M TAKING THE FIRST flight out," Jordan said without preamble when he called Dana back. "I'll let you know what time I arrive so you can pick me up at the airport."

Dana bit down on her tongue, determined not to let him get to her. He seemed to just assume she wouldn't have anything else to do but pick him up at Gallatin Field, a good fifty miles away. "Jordan, you must have forgotten. I have a job."

"You're half owner of a…fabric shop. Don't tell me you can't get away."

She wasn't going to chauffeur him around the whole time he was here, or worse, let him commandeer her vehicle. She took a breath. She would have loved to have lost her temper and told him just what she thought of him. He was in no position to be asking anything of her.

She let out the breath. "You'll have to rent a car, Jordan. I'll be working." A thought struck her like the back of a hand. "Where will you be staying in case I need to reach you?" Not with her. Please not with her at the ranch.

She heard the knife edge in his voice. "Don't worry, I'm not going to stay at that old run-down ranch house with you."

She almost slumped with relief. She'd suspected for some time that he was in financial trouble. Ever since two years ago when he'd married Jill, an out-of-work model, Jordan had seemed desperate for money.

"I assume Jill is coming with you?" Dana said, assuming just the opposite.

"Jill can't make it this time."

"Oh?" Dana bit her tongue again, just not quick enough. Jill had set foot in Montana only once and found it too backwoodsy.

"You have something to say, Dana? We all know what an authority you are on romantic relationships."

The jab felt all the more painful given that Hud was back in town. "At least I had the sense not to marry him." Instantly she wished she could snatch back the words. "Jordan, I don't want to fight with you." It was true. She hated how quickly this had escalated into something ugly. "Let's not do this."

"No, Dana, you brought it up," Jordan said. "If you have something to say, let's hear it."

"Jordan, you know this isn't what Mom wanted, us fighting like this."

He let out a cruel laugh. "You think I care what she wanted? The only thing she ever loved was that damned ranch. And just like her, you chose it over a man."

"Mom didn't choose the ranch over Dad," Dana said. "She tried to make their marriage work. It was Dad who—"

"Don't be naive, Dana. She drove him away. The same way you did Hud."

She wasn't going to discuss this with him. Especially today. Especially with Hud back. "I have to go, Jordan."

He didn't seem to hear her. "At least I have someone to warm my bed at night. Can your precious ranch do that?"

"Enjoy it while it lasts," Dana snapped. "Jill will be long gone once you don't have anything else you can pillage to appease her."

She knew at once that she'd gone too far. Jordan had never liked to hear the truth.

Dana smacked herself on the forehead, wishing she could take back the angry words. He'd always known how to push her buttons. Isn't that what siblings were especially adept at because they knew each other's weaknesses so well?

"Jordan, I'm sorry," she said, meaning it.

"I'll have Dad pick me up. But, dear sister, I will deal with you when I see you. And at least buy a damned answering machine." He ended the call abruptly.

She felt dirty, as if she'd been wrestling in the mud as she hung up. She hadn't wanted the conversation to end like that. It would only make matters worse once he hit town.

She told herself that with luck maybe she wouldn't have to see him. She wouldn't have to see any of her siblings. The only one she'd been even a little close to was Clay, the youngest, but she wasn't even talking to *him* lately.

And she didn't want an answering machine. Anyone who needed to reach her, would. Eventually. She could just imagine the kind of messages Jordan would leave her.

She shuddered at the thought. As bad as she felt about the argument and her angry words, she was relieved. At least Jordan wasn't staying at the ranch, she thought with a rueful smile as she went into the kitchen and poured herself a glass of wine.

As she did, she heard the sound of a vehicle coming up the road to the house and groaned. Now what?

Glancing out the window she saw the marshal's black SUV barreling toward her.

This day just kept getting better.

Chapter Four

Across the river and a half mile back up a wide valley, the Cardwell ranch house sat against a backdrop of granite cliffs and towering dark pines. The house was a big, two-story rambling affair with a wide front porch and a new brick-red metal roof.

Behind it stood a huge weathered barn and some outbuildings and corrals. The dark shapes loomed out of the falling snow and darkness as Hud swung the SUV into the ranch yard.

He shut off the engine. Out of habit, he looked up at Dana's bedroom window. There was nothing but darkness behind the glass but in his mind he could see her waving to him as she'd done so many times years before.

As he got out of the patrol car, ducking deep into his coat against the falling snow, he ran to the porch, half expecting Dana's mother, Mary Justice Cardwell, to answer the door. Mary had been a ranch woman through and through. No one had ever understood why she'd married Angus Cardwell. He'd been too handsome and charming for his own good, with little ambition and even less regard for ranch work. But he'd also been heir to the C-Bar Ranch adjacent to the Justice Ranch.

When the two had married, so had the ranches. The combined spread became the Cardwell Ranch.

No one had been surprised when the two divorced. Or when Angus gave up the ranch to Mary.

People were just surprised that the two stayed together long enough to have four children.

And Angus and Mary had certainly produced beautiful children.

Jordan, the oldest, was almost too good-looking and had definitely taken after his father. Clay was the youngest, a slim, quiet young man who worked in local theater groups.

Then there was Stacy, two years older than Dana, cheerleader cute. Stacy had cashed in on her looks her whole life, trading up in three marriages so far. He didn't like to think about Stacy.

There was no comparison between the two sisters. While Dana also had the Justice-Cardwell good looks, she had something more going for her. She'd been the good student, the hard worker, the one who wanted to carry on the family tradition at the ranch, while the others had cut and run the first chance they got.

Dana, like her mother, loved everything about ranching. It and breathing were one and the same to her. That's why he couldn't understand why Dana would be selling the place. It scared him.

He couldn't stand the thought that he'd come back too late. Or worse that he'd been carrying a torch for a woman who no longer existed.

As he started to knock, he heard a dog growl and looked over to see a gray-muzzled, white-and-liver springer spaniel.

"Joe?" He couldn't believe his eyes. He knelt as the dog lumbered over to him, tail wagging with recognition. "Joe, hey, old boy. I didn't think you'd still be around." He petted the dog, happy to see a friendly face from the past.

"Was there something you wanted?"

He hadn't heard the front door open. Dana stood leaning against the frame, a glass of wine in her hand and a look that said she was in no mood for whatever he was selling.

He wished like hell that he wasn't going to add to her troubles. "Evening," he said, tipping his hat as he gave Joe a pat and straightened. "Mind if I come in for a few minutes? I need to talk to you."

"If this has something to do with you and me…"

"No." He gave her a rueful smile. There was no "you and me"—not anymore. Not ever again from the look in her brown eyes. "It's about what we found in the well."

All the starch seemed to go out of her. She stepped back, motioning him in.

He took off his hat and stepped in to slip off his boots and his jacket before following her through the very Western living area with its stone and wood to the bright, big airy kitchen. Joe followed at his heels.

"Have a seat."

Hud pulled out a chair at the large worn oak table, put his Stetson on an adjacent chair and sat.

Dana frowned as Joe curled up at his feet. "Traitor," she mouthed at the dog.

Hud looked around, memories of all the times he'd sat in this kitchen threatening to drown him. Mary Justice Cardwell at the stove making dinner, Dana helping, all of them chatting about the goings-on at the ranch, a new foal, a broken down tractor, cows to be moved. He could almost smell the roast and homemade rolls baking and hear Dana's laughter, see the secret, knowing looks she'd sent him, feel the warmth of being a part of this family.

And Dana would have made her mother's double chocolate brownies for dessert—especially for him.

Dana set a bottle of wine and a glass in front of him, putting it down a little too hard and snapping him back to the present. "Unless you think we're both going to need something stronger?" she asked.

"Wine will do." He poured himself some and topped off her glass as she took a chair across from him. She curled her bare feet under her but not before he noticed that her toenails were painted coral. She wore jeans and an autumn gold sweater that hugged her curves and lit her eyes.

He lifted his glass, but words failed him as he looked at her. The faint scent of her wafted over to him as she took a drink of her wine. She'd always smelled of summer to him, an indefinable scent that filled his heart like helium.

Feeling awkward, he took another drink, his throat tight. He'd known being in this house again would bring it all back. It did. But just being here alone with Dana, not being able to touch her or to say all the things he wanted to say to her, was killing him. She didn't want to hear his excuses. Hell, clearly she'd hoped to never lay eyes on him again.

But a part of him, he knew, was still hoping she'd been the one who'd sent him the anonymous note that had brought him back.

"So what did you find in the well?" she asked as if she wanted this over with as quickly as possible. She took another sip of wine, watching him over the rim of her glass, her eyes growing dark with a rage born of pain that he recognized only too well.

Dana hadn't sent the note. He'd only been fooling himself. She still believed he'd betrayed her.

"The bones are human but you already knew that," he said, finding his voice.

She nodded, waiting.

"We won't know for certain until Rupert calls from the crime lab, but his opinion is that the body belonged to a Caucasian woman between the ages of twenty-eight and thirty-five and that she's been down there about fifteen years." He met her gaze and saw the shock register.

"Only fifteen years?"

Hud nodded. It seemed that, like him, she'd hoped the bones were very old and had no recent connection to their lives.

Dana let out a breath. "How did she get there?"

"She was murdered. Rupert thinks she was thrown down the well and then shot."

Dana sat up, her feet dropping to the floor with a slap. "No." She set the wineglass down on the table, the wine almost spilling.

Without thinking, Hud reached over to steady the glass, steady her. His fingers brushed hers. She jerked her hand back as if he'd sliced her fingers with a knife.

He pulled back his hand and picked up his wineglass, wishing now that he'd asked for something stronger.

Dana was sitting back in the chair, her arms crossed, feet on the floor. She looked shaken. He wondered how much of it was from what he'd told her about the bones in the well and how much from his touch. Did she ever wonder what their lives might have been like if she hadn't broken off the engagement? They would be husband and wife now. Something he always thought about. It never failed to bring a wave of regret with it.

He didn't tell Dana that the woman had still been alive, maybe even calling to her attacker for help as he left her down there.

"I'm going to have to question your family and anyone else who had access to the property or who might have known about the dry well," he said.

She didn't seem to hear him. Her gaze went to the large window. Outside, the snow fell in huge feathery flakes, obscuring the mountains. "What was she shot with?"

He hesitated, then said, "Rupert thinks it was a .38." He waited a beat before he added, "Does your father still have that .38 of his?"

She seemed startled by the question, her gaze flying back to him. "I have no idea. Why—" Her look turned to stone. "You can't really believe—"

"Do you have any guns in the house?" he asked in his official tone.

Her eyes narrowed in reaction. "Just the double-barreled shotgun by the door. But you're welcome to search the house if you don't believe me."

He remembered the shotgun. Mary Justice Cardwell had kept it by the door, loaded with buckshot, to chase away bears from her chicken coop.

"You have any idea who this woman in the well might have been?" he asked.

"Fifteen years ago I was sixteen." She met his gaze. Something hot flashed there as if she, too, remembered her sixteenth birthday and their first kiss.

"You recall a woman going missing about that time?" he asked, his voice sounding strange to his ears.

She shook her head, her gaze never leaving his face. "Won't there be a missing person's report?"

"The law and justice center fire in Bozeman destroyed all the records twelve years ago," he said.

"So we might never know who she was?" Dana asked.

"Maybe not. But if she was local, someone might remember her." He pulled his notebook and pen from his pocket. "I'm going to need Jordan's phone number so I can contact him."

"He's flying in tomorrow. He'll probably stay with Angus, but I'm sure he'll be contacting you."

He thought it strange she referred to her father as Angus. He wondered what had been going on in the years he'd been gone.

"You know where to find them," she continued. "Angus on the nearest bar stool. Clay at his studio in the old Emerson in Bozeman. And Stacy—" Her voice broke. "Well, she's where you left her."

Hud surprised himself by taking the jab without flinching.

"I was really sorry to hear about your mom's accident." He'd heard that Mary had been bucked off a horse and suffered severe brain damage. She'd lived for a short while, but never regained consciousness.

Dana locked eyes with him. "She always liked you." She said it as if it was the one mistake her mother ever made.

"Is that why you're selling the ranch?"

She got up from the table. "Is there anything else?"

He could see that he shouldn't have mentioned the sale. Not only was it none of his business, but he also got the feeling today really wasn't the day to ask.

He finished his wine and pushed himself up from the chair. Picking up his Stetson, he settled it on his head. "I see you forgot your ring again."

DANA CURSED HERSELF for ever lying about the engagement let alone the ring. "The stone was loose," she said, compounding the lies. She'd spent thirty-one years telling the truth and Hud came back to town and she became an instant liar.

"You're not engaged to Lanny Rankin," he said softly. "Are you?"

She lifted her chin ready to defend her lie to the death. "Not that it's any of your business—"

"Why did you lie to me, Dana?"

Something in his tone stopped her cold. Obviously he thought she'd done it to make him jealous because she still cared. This was turning out to be the worst day of her life.

"I didn't want you thinking there was any chance for you and me."

He smiled. "Oh, your attitude toward me made that pretty clear. You didn't have to come up with a fiancé." His eyes suddenly narrowed. "Why *hasn't* the guy asked you to marry him? Something wrong with him?"

"No," she snapped. "My relationship with Lanny is none of your business." She could see the wheels turning in his stubborn head. He thought more than ever that she was still carrying a torch for him.

"You're the most annoying man I've ever known," she said as she headed for the door to show him out.

His soft chuckle chased after her, piercing her heart with memory. So many memories of the two of them together.

"At least I still have that distinction," he said as she snatched open the front door and he stepped through it.

Joe, she noticed, had followed them and now stood by her feet. The old dog might be deaf and barely getting around anymore, but he was no fool. When push came to shove, he knew where his loyalties lay.

Hud turned in the doorway to look at her, all humor gone from his expression. "At some point,

I'll need to talk to you about this investigation. I can come here or you can come down to the Big Sky office—"

"The office would be fine," she said. "Just let me know when."

"Dana, I really am sorry about—" he waved a hand "—everything."

Her smile felt as sharp as a blade. "Good night, Hud." She closed the door in his face but not before she heard him say, "Good night, Dana," the way he used to say it after they'd kissed.

She leaned against the door, her knees as weak as water. Dammit, she wasn't going to cry. She'd shed too many tears for Hud Savage. He wasn't getting even one more out of her.

But she felt hot tears course down her cheeks. She wiped at the sudden wetness, biting her lip to keep from breaking down and bawling. What a lousy day this had been. This birthday was destined to go down as the worst.

Joe let out a bark, his old eyes on her, tail wagging.

"I'm not mad at you," she said, and squatted to wrap her arms around him. "I know you always liked Hud. Didn't we all?"

Dana had never been one to wallow in self-pity. At least not for long. She'd gone on with her life after Hud left. His coming back now wasn't going to send her into another tailspin.

She rose and walked to the kitchen window, drawn to it by what she now knew had been in the old well all these years. The horror of it sent a shudder through her. Was it possible she had known the woman? Or worse, she thought, with a jolt, that Angus had? Hud had reminded her that her father had owned a .38.

With a groan, she recalled the time her father had let her and Hud shoot tin cans off the ranch fence with the gun.

Through the falling snow, she looked toward the hillside and hugged herself against the chill of her thoughts before glancing at the kitchen clock.

There was time if she hurried. She'd heard that her dad and uncle were playing with their band at the Corral Bar tonight. If she left now she might be able to talk to both of them and still get back in time for her date with Lanny.

She was anxious to talk to her father—before he and her uncle had time to come up with a convincing story. The thought surprised her. Why had she just assumed he had something to hide? Because, she thought with a rueful grin, he was her father and she knew him.

By now the canyon grapevine would be humming with the news about the body in the well. After all, Jordan had heard all the way back in New York City.

She'd just have to weather the blizzard—the storm outside as well as the arrival of her brother tomorrow from New York.

She groaned at the thought as she took her coat from a hook by the door. It was a good ten miles down the road to the bar and the roads would be slick, the visibility poor. But she knew she wouldn't be able to get any sleep until she talked to her father.

She just hoped it was early enough for him to be halfway sober, but she wasn't counting on it.

As Hud drove away from the ranch, he kept saying the words over and over in her head.

She isn't engaged. She isn't engaged.

He smiled to himself. Admittedly, it was a small victory. But he'd been right. She wasn't engaged to Lanny.

Maybe even after all this time, he knew Dana better than she'd thought.

As snow continued to fall, he drove across the narrow bridge that spanned the Gallatin River and turned onto Highway 191 headed south down the Gallatin Canyon, feeling better than he had in years.

The "canyon," as it was known, ran from the mouth just south of Gallatin Gateway almost to West Yellowstone, ninety miles of winding road that trailed the river in a deep cut through the steep mountains on each side.

It had changed a lot since Hud was a boy. Luxury houses had sprouted up all around the resort. Fortunately some of the original cabins still remained and the majority of the canyon was national forest so it would always remain undeveloped.

The drive along the river had always been breathtaking, a winding strip of highway that followed the river up over the Continental Divide and down the other side to West Yellowstone.

Hud had rented a cabin a few miles up the canyon from Big Sky. But as he started up the highway, his headlights doing little to cut through the thick falling snow, his radio squawked.

He pulled over into one of the wide spots along the river. "Savage here."

The dispatcher in Bozeman, an elderly woman named Lorraine, announced she was patching through a call.

"Marshal Savage?" asked a voice he didn't recognize. "This is Dr. Gerald Cross with the crime lab in Missoula."

"Yes." Hud wondered why it wasn't Rupert calling.

"I have information on the evidence you sent us that I thought you'd want to hear about right away." There was the fluttering sound of papers, then the doctor's voice again. "We got lucky. Normally something like this takes weeks if not months, but your coroner was so insistent that we run the tests ASAP... The bullet lodged in the skull of the victim matches a bullet used in a shooting in your area."

Hud blinked in confusion. "What shooting?"

Another shuffle of papers. "A Judge Raymond Randolph. He was murdered in his home. An apparent robbery?"

Hud felt the air rush from his lungs. Judge Randolph. And the night Hud had been trying to forget for the past five years.

He cleared his throat. "You're saying the same gun that killed the Jane Doe from the well was used in the Randolph case?"

"The striations match. No doubt about it. Same gun used for both murders," the doctor said.

"The Randolph case was only five years ago. Hasn't this body been down in the well longer than that? The coroner estimated about fifteen years."

"Our preliminary findings support that time period," Dr. Cross said.

Hud tried to take it in: two murders, years apart, but the same gun was used for both?

"We found further evidence in the dirt that was recovered around the body," the doctor was saying. "An emerald ring. The good news is that it was custom-made by a jeweler in your area. Should be easy to track."

Hud felt hopeful. "Can you fax me the information on the ring along with digital photos?"

"I'll have that done right away," the doctor said. "Also, three fingers on her left hand were broken, the ring finger in two places. Broken in the fall, I would assume, unless she tried to fight off her assailant.

"But what also might be helpful in identifying the woman is the prior break in the Jane Doe's radius, right wrist," the doctor continued. "It appears it was broken and healed shortly before her death. The break had been set, indicating she sought medical attention. She would have been wearing a cast in the weeks prior to her death."

A woman with a broken wrist in a cast.

"I've sent the information to both the dentists and doctors in your area," Dr. Cross said. "All her teeth were intact and she'd had dental work done on several molars not long before her death, as well. You got lucky on this one."

Lucky? Hud didn't feel lucky. Again he wondered why Rupert hadn't made the call. "Is Dr. Milligan still there? I wanted to ask him something."

"Sorry, but Rupert left some time ago. He said he had an appointment."

Hud thanked him and hung up the radio, wondering what was going on with Rupert. Why hadn't he been the one to call? It wasn't like him. Especially since he'd been right about everything. He would have called if for nothing else than to say, "Good thing you didn't bet me."

Because, Hud thought, Rupert wanted to get the information to someone else first? For instance, his friend the former marshal, Brick Savage?

Hud stared out at the falling snow. The night was bright, the scene past the windshield a tableau of varying shades of white and gray. Next to him the Gallatin River ran under a thick layer of ice. He couldn't remember ever feeling this cold.

He reached over and kicked up the heat, letting the vent blow into his face.

The same gun used to murder the woman in a red dress was used during what had appeared to be a robbery of Judge Randolph's residence. The judge had been shot and killed—the two incidents years apart.

Hud rubbed his hand over his face. No, he didn't feel lucky in the least. Judge Randolph had been one of Brick Savage's most outspoken opponents. Hud had never known what had spurred the judge's hatred of Marshal Brick Savage. The two had butted heads on more than one occasion, but then his father butted heads with a lot of people, Hud thought.

The difference was the judge had been in a position to make his threats come true. There had been talk that Judge Randolph was determined to see Marshal Brick Savage fired.

If the judge hadn't met such an untimely demise, who knows what would have happened, Hud thought as he pulled back onto the highway, the snow falling now in a dizzying white blur.

He hadn't been looking forward to going back to the cabin he'd rented near Big Sky. The cabin was small with just the bare essentials—exactly what he'd thought he wanted.

Except tonight he had too much on his mind to go back there yet. He turned around and headed for Bozeman. He wouldn't be able to sleep until he looked at the case file on Judge Raymond Randolph's robbery-murder.

He thought again about the anonymous note he'd received. Someone had wanted him back here. Someone with an agenda of their own?

As he drove down the canyon, the snow falling in a blinding wall of white, he feared he was being manipulated—just as he'd been five years ago.

Chapter Five

Dana brushed snow from her coat as she pushed open the door to the Corral Bar. The scent of beer and smoke hit her as she stepped in, pulled off her hat and, shaking the snow from it, looked around the bar for her father.

It was early. The place was relatively empty, only a few locals at the bar and a half-dozen others in booths eating the burgers the Corral was famous for.

A country-western song played on the jukebox, competing with the hum of conversation. The bartender was busy talking with a couple at her end of the bar.

Dana spotted her father and uncle at the far end on adjacent stools. They each had two beers in front of them and hadn't seemed to notice her come in. That was because they had their heads together in deep conversation.

As she approached, she saw her father look up and catch her reflection in the mirror. He sat up straighter, pulling back but mouthing something to Harlan as if warning him of her approach. Uncle Harlan turned on his stool to flash her a smile, both men appearing nervous. Clearly she had interrupted something.

"Dana," Harlan said, sounding surprised. "Haven't seen you for a while." Like his brother, he was a big man with a head of dark hair peppered with gray.

"Uncle Harlan." She patted his arm as she passed, her gaze on her father.

While Angus Cardwell resembled his brother, he'd definitely gotten the looks in the family. He'd been a devastatingly handsome young man and Dana could see why her mother had fallen for him.

Angus was still handsome and would have been quite the catch in the canyon if it wasn't for his love of alcohol. Thanks to the healthy settlement he'd received from Dana's mother in the divorce, he didn't have to work.

"How's my baby girl?" Angus asked, and leaned over to kiss her cheek. She smelled the familiar scent of beer on his breath. "Happy birthday."

Dana had always been his baby girl and still was— even at thirty-one. "Fine. Thank you.

"Is there someplace we could talk for a minute?" she asked. Angus shot a look at Harlan.

"We could probably step into the back room," her father said. "I'm sure Bob wouldn't mind." Bob owned the place and since Angus was likely the most regular of the regulars who frequented the bar, Bob probably wouldn't mind.

"Guess I'll tag along," Uncle Harlan said, already sliding off his stool.

The back room was part office, part spare room. It had a small desk and an office chair along with a threadbare overstuffed chair and a sofa that looked like it might pull out into a bed. The room smelled of stale cigarette smoke and beer.

"So what's up?" Angus asked. Both he and Harlan had brought along their beers.

She studied them for a moment, then said, "I'm sure you've heard about what happened at the ranch today." She could see by their expressions that they had.

"Hell of a thing," Angus said.

Harlan nodded in agreement and tipped his beer bottle to his lips.

"Any idea how the bones got into our well?" she asked, wondering how much they'd heard on the canyon grapevine.

"Us?" Harlan said, looking puzzled. "Why would we know anything about her?"

Her. So they'd heard it was a woman. She couldn't believe how quickly word spread.

She hadn't meant to sound so accusing. "I just thought you might have some idea since you were both on the ranch during that time." Her parents were still together then, kind of, and her uncle had been working on the ranch and living in one of the spare bedrooms.

A look passed between them.

"What?" she asked.

"We were just talking about this," her father said.

"And?" she prodded.

"And nothing," Angus said.

"Anyone could have come onto the ranch and done it," Harlan said. "Could have driven right by the house or come in the back on one of the old loggin' roads. Could have been anyone." He looked embarrassed, as if he'd spoken out of turn. Or maybe said too much. He took a drink of his beer.

"So you two have it all figured out," she said, studying them. "That mean you've figured out who she was? Seems she went into the well about fifteen years ago."

"Fifteen years?" Clearly, Angus was surprised by that.

"Bunch of cowhands on the ranch back then," Harlan said. "Anyone could have known about the well. There's old wells and mine shafts all over Montana. Usually an old foundation nearby. Not that hard to find if you're looking for one."

Dana thought about the homestead chimney still standing and part of the foundation visible from the ranch house. Stood to reason, she supposed, there would be an old well nearby.

"All this seasonal help around here, the woman didn't have to be a local," Harlan said. "She could have been working in the canyon for the summer or even at the ski hill for the winter."

"Wouldn't someone have missed her, though?" Dana said, noticing her father was nursing his beer and saying little.

Harlan shrugged. "If she had family. If her family knew where she'd gone to in the first place. You know how these kids are who show up for the seasonal employment. Most move on within a few weeks. Could have been a runaway even. Wasn't there some bones found in the canyon a few years ago and they never did find out who that guy was?"

She nodded. The other remains that had been found were male and no identification had ever been made. Was the same thing going to happen with the woman's bones from the well?

She started to ask her father about his .38, but changed her mind. "You all right?" she asked her father.

Angus smiled and tossed his now empty beer bottle into the trash. "Fine, baby girl. I just hate to see you upset over this. How about I buy you a drink to celebrate your birthday and we talk about something else?" he asked as he opened the door to the bar. The blare of the jukebox swept in along with a blue haze of smoke and the smell of burgers and beer.

Dana met his gaze. His eyes were shiny with alcohol and something else. Whatever he was hiding, he was keeping it to himself whether she liked it or not.

"Maybe some other time," she said. "I have a date tonight."

"I heard Hud was back," he said, and grinned at her.

"I'm not with Hud, Dad." How many times did she have to tell him that she was never getting back together with Hud? "Lanny's taking me out to dinner for my birthday."

"Oh," Angus said. He'd never been fond of Lanny Rankin and she'd never understood why. All her father had ever said was, "I just don't think he's the right man for you."

AT THE LAW AND JUSTICE CENTER, Hud sat with the file on the Judge Raymond Randolph killing, still haunted by that night. Most of the night was nothing but a black hole in his memory. He couldn't account for too many hours and had spent years trying to remember what he'd done that night.

He shook his head. It was one of the questions he was bound and determined to get answered now that he was back in Montana.

How strange that his first case as acting Gallatin Canyon marshal was tied to that night. Coincidence? He had to wonder.

He opened the file. Since he'd left town right after the judge's death, he knew little about the case.

The first thing that hit him was the sight of his father's notes neatly printed on sheets of eight-and-a-half-by-eleven, lined white paper. Brick Savage had never learned to type.

Hud felt a chill at just the sight of his father's neat printing, the writing short and to the point.

The judge had been at his annual Toastmasters dinner; his wife, Katherine "Kitty" Randolph, was away visiting her sister in Butte. The judge had returned home early, reason unknown, and was believed to have interrupted an alleged robbery in progress. He was shot twice, point-blank in the heart with a .38-caliber pistol.

A neighbor heard the shots and called the sheriff's department. A young new deputy by the name of Hudson Savage was on duty that night. But when he couldn't be reached, Marshal Brick Savage took the call.

Hud felt his hands begin to shake. He'd known he was going to have to face that night again when he'd come back, but seeing it in black-and-white rattled him more than he wanted to admit.

Brick reported that as he neared the Randolph house, he spotted two suspects fleeing the residence. He gave chase. The high-speed chase ended near what was known as the 35-mile-an-hour curve, one of the worst sections in the winding canyon road because it ended in a bridge and another curve in the opposite direction.

The suspect driving the car lost control after which the car rolled several times before coming to a stop upside down in the middle of the Gallatin River.

Both the driver and the passenger were killed.

Marshal Brick Savage called for an ambulance, wrecker and the coroner before returning to the Randolph house where he discovered signs of a break-in and the judge lying dead in the foyer.

According to Brick's account, evidence was later found in the suspects' car that connected the two to the robbery-murder. The suspects were Ty and Mason Kirk, two local brothers who had been in trouble pretty much all of their lives.

The case seemed cut-and-dried. Except now the murder weapon appeared to have been used in the murder of a woman in a well a good decade before.

Tired and discouraged, he photocopied the file and drove back up the canyon. Still, he couldn't face the small cabin he'd rented. Not yet.

He drove to his office in the deepening snow. His headlights shone on the evergreens along each side of the road, their branches bent under the weight of the snowfall. A white silence had filled the night. The streets were so quiet, he felt as if there wasn't another soul within miles as he neared his office.

Had he made a terrible mistake coming back here, taking the job as marshal even temporarily? It had been instantaneous. When he'd gotten the offer, he'd said yes without a moment's hesitation, thinking it was fate. After the note he'd received, he was coming back anyway. But to have a job. Not just a job, but the job he'd always said he wanted....

He pulled up to the office, turned off the engine and lights, and sat for a moment in the snowy darkness, trying to put his finger on what was bothering him.

Something about the Judge Raymond Randolph murder case. Something was wrong. He could feel it deep in his bones, like a sliver buried under the skin.

As he picked up the copied file from the seat next to him, he had that same sick feeling he'd had when he'd looked down into the dry well and seen human bones.

IT WASN'T UNTIL DANA returned home from the bar that she noticed the tracks on the porch. She stopped and turned to look back out through the falling snow.

Someone had been here. The tire tracks had filled with snow and were barely visible. That's why she hadn't noticed them on her way in. Plus she'd had other things on her mind.

But now, standing on the porch, she saw the boot tracks where someone had come to the door. She checked her watch. Too early for it to have been Lanny.

Her breath caught in her throat as she realized the tracks went right into the house. She'd never locked the front door in her life. Just as she hadn't tonight. This was rural Montana. No one locked their doors.

Carefully she touched the knob. It was cold even through her gloves. The door swung open.

The living room looked just as she'd left it. Except for a few puddles of melted snow where someone had gone inside. Her heart rate tripled as she trailed the wet footprints across the floor to the kitchen.

That's when she saw it. A small wrapped package on the kitchen table.

A birthday present. Her relief was quickly replaced by anger. She had a pretty good idea who'd left it. Hud. He'd returned and, knowing the door would be unlocked, had come in and left it.

Damn him. Why did he have to come back? Tears burned her eyes. She wouldn't cry. She…would…not…cry.

Her heart was still pounding too hard, the tears too close after the day she'd had. She turned on the lights, shrugged out of her coat to hang it on the hook by the door and wiped angrily at her eyes. *Damn you, Hud.*

She had to get ready for her date. Stumbling up the stairs, she went to the bathroom, stripped down and stepped into the shower. She turned her face up to the water for a moment. The memory of the Hud she'd loved filled her with a pain that almost doubled her over. A sob broke loose, opening the dam. Leaning against the shower stall she couldn't hold back the pain any longer. It came in a flood. She was helpless to stop it.

After a while she got control again, finished showering and got out. She'd have to take care of the package on the kitchen table. She quickly dressed. Her eyes were red from crying, her face flushed. She dug in the drawer looking for makeup she seldom if ever wore, but it did little to hide her swollen eyes.

The doorbell rang. Lanny was early. She'd hoped to get back downstairs and throw away Hud's birthday present before Lanny arrived.

She ran downstairs without glancing toward the kitchen and Hud's present, unhooking her coat from the hook as she opened the door and flipped on the porch light.

Lanny looked up from where he stood about to ring the doorbell again. He was tall and slim with sandy-colored hair and thick-lashed brown eyes. Any woman with good eyesight would agree he was handsome. Even Dana.

But she'd never felt that thumpity-thump in her pulse when she saw him. She didn't go weak in the knees when they kissed, hardly thought about him when they were apart.

She enjoyed his company when they were together, which over the past five years hadn't been very often. Her fault. She'd put Lanny off for a long time after Hud left because she hadn't been ready to date. And then she'd been busy much of the time.

She'd thought that in time she would feel about him the way he felt about her. She'd wished she could feel more for him, especially after he'd confessed that he'd had a crush on her since first grade.

"So it's true," he said, now looking into her face.

She knew her eyes were still red, her face puffy from crying and she'd done enough lying for one day. "It's been a rough birthday."

"It's all over town," Lanny said. "According to the rumor mill, you and I've been upgraded."

She groaned. Hud must have asked someone about the engagement. That's all it would take to get the rumor going. "Sorry. I got a little carried away."

He nodded ruefully. "Then it's not true?"

She shook her head and saw the hurt in his expression. For the first time she had to admit to herself that no matter how long she dated Lanny, she was never going to fall in love with him. She'd only been kidding herself. And giving Lanny false hope. She couldn't keep doing that.

"I figured I'd probably have heard if it was true," he said. "But you never know."

Yeah, she did know. "I'm sorry," she said again, unable to think of anything else to say. She hated to break it off tonight. He would think she was going back to Hud and that's the last rumor she wanted circulating. But she had to get it over with. She didn't think it would come as too big of a surprise to Lanny.

"You still want to go out tonight?" he asked, as if he sensed what was coming.

"Nothing's changed," she said too quickly.

"Yeah, that's kind of the problem, huh?" He glanced into the house.

She didn't want to have this discussion here, on her doorstep, and she didn't want to invite him inside. She didn't want him to see the present Hud had left her. It would only hurt him worse and that was something she didn't want to do.

"Ready?" she asked.

Lanny hesitated for only a moment, then walked her through the falling snow to his large SUV.

She chattered on about the weather, then the sewing shop and Hilde, finally running out of safe conversation as he pulled into the restaurant.

Once inside, Dana found herself watching the door. She couldn't help it. Now that she knew Hud was back in the canyon, she expected to run into him at every turn, which kept him on her mind. Damn him.

"Hud's working late tonight," Lanny said.

She jerked her head around. "I wasn't—" The beginning of a lie died on her lips. "I just hate running into him," she said sheepishly.

Lanny nodded, his smile indulgent. "After all this time, it must be a shock, him coming back." He wiped a line of sweat off his water glass, not looking at her. "He say what brought him back?"

"No." That was one of the things that bothered her. Why after so long?

"He must think he has a chance with you." He met her gaze.

"Well, he doesn't." She picked up her menu, the words swimming in front of her. "What did Sally say was the special tonight?"

Lanny reached over and pulled down the menu so he could see her face. "I need you to be honest with me," he said, his voice low even though because of the weather there were only a couple of people in the restaurant and they weren't close by.

She nodded, her throat a desert.

"Dana, I thought you'd gotten over Hud. I thought after he hurt you the way he did, you'd never want to see him again. Am I wrong about that or—" He looked past her, his expression telling her before she turned that Hud had come into the restaurant.

Her heart took off at a gallop at just the sight of him. She looked to see if he was alone, afraid he wouldn't be. He was. He stepped up to the counter and started to sit down, instantly changing his mind when he saw her and Lanny.

"You need a table, Hud?" Sally asked him from behind the counter.

"Nah, just wanted to get a burger," he said, turning his back to Dana and Lanny. "Working late tonight."

Dana recalled now that Lanny had said Hud was working tonight. How had he known that?

"Working, huh," Sally said, glancing toward Dana's table. "You want fries with that?" She chuckled. "Daddy always said if I didn't pay more attention in school I'd be saying that. He was right."

"No fries. Just the burger." He sat at the counter, his shoulders hunched, head down. Dana felt her traitorous heart weaken at the sight. She'd thought she wanted to hurt him, hurt him badly, the way he'd hurt her. Seeing her on a date with Lanny was killing him. She should have taken pleasure in that.

Sally must have seen his discomfort. "You know I can have that sent over to you since you have work to do."

"I'd appreciate that," he said, getting up quickly, his relief so apparent it made Dana hurt. He laid some money on the counter and, without looking in her direction, pulled his coat collar up around his neck as he stepped out into the snowstorm.

A gust of winter washed through the restaurant and he was gone. Just like that. Just like five years ago. Dana felt that same emptiness, that same terrible loss.

"We don't have to do this," Lanny said as she turned back to the table and him.

Her heart ached and her eyes burned. "I'm sorry."

"Please, stop apologizing," Lanny snapped, then softened his expression. "You and I have spent too long apologizing for how we feel."

"Can we just have dinner as friends?" she asked.

His smile never reached his eyes. "Sure. Friends. Why not? Two friends having dinner." The words hit her like thrown stones. Anger burned in his gaze as he picked up his menu.

"Lanny—"

"It's your birthday, Dana. Let's not say anything to spoil it."

She almost laughed. Her birthday had been spoiled from the moment she'd opened her eyes this morning.

They ordered, then sat in silence until Sally arrived with their salads.

Dana felt terrible on so many levels. She just wanted to get through this dinner. She asked him about his work and got him talking a little.

But by the time they left, they'd exhausted all topics of conversation. Lanny said nothing on the drive back to the ranch. He didn't offer to walk her to her door.

"Goodbye, Dana," he said, and waited for her to get out of the car. He met her gaze for an instant in the yard light and she saw rage burning in his eyes.

There was nothing she could say. She opened her door. "Thank you for dinner."

He nodded without looking at her and she got out, hurrying through the falling snow to the porch before she turned to watch him drive away.

It wasn't until she entered the house that she remembered the present on her kitchen table.

The box, the size of a thick paperback book, was wrapped in red foil. There was a red bow on top with a tag that read Happy Birthday!

She knew exactly what was inside—which gave her every reason not to touch it. But still she picked up the box, disappointed in herself.

She felt the weight of the chocolates inside, felt the weight of their lost love. She'd tried to get over Hud. Tried so hard. Why did he have to come back and remind her of everything—including how much she had loved him?

Still loved him.

All the old feelings rained down on her like a summer downpour, drowning her in regret.

Damn Hud.

She set the box down, heard the chocolates rattle inside. Not just any chocolate. Only the richest, most wonderful, hard-to-find chocolates in the world. These chocolates were dark and creamy and melted the instant they touched your tongue. These chocolates made you close your eyes and moan and were right up there with sex. Well, not sex with Hud. Nothing could beat that.

Making love with Hud was a whole other experience—and she hated him even more now for reminding her of it.

Knowing her weakness, Hud had found these amazing chocolates and had given them to her on her twenty-fifth birthday—the night he'd asked her to marry him.

She glared down at the box and, like niggling at a sore tooth with her tongue, she reminded herself of how Hud had betrayed her five years ago. That did the trick.

Grabbing up the box of chocolates, she stormed over to the trash. The container was empty except for the balled up card from her sister that she'd retrieved from the floor and thrown away. She dropped the box of chocolates into the clean, white plastic trash bag, struck by how appropriate it was that the card from Stacy and the chocolates from Hud ended up together in the trash.

The chocolates rattled again when they hit the bottom of the bag and for just a moment she was tempted. What would it hurt to eat one? Or even two? Hud would never have to know.

No, that's exactly what he was counting on. That she wouldn't be able to resist the chocolates—just as there was a time when she couldn't resist him.

Angrily she slammed the cupboard door. He'd broken her heart in the worst possible way and if he thought he could worm his way back in, he was sadly mistaken.

She stormed over to the phone and called his office.

"Hello?"

"It didn't work," she said, her voice cracking. Tears burned her eyes. She made a swipe at them.

"Dana?"

"Your…present… The one you left me after sneaking into my house like a thief. It didn't work. I threw the chocolates away."

"Dana." His voice sounded strange. "I didn't give you a present."

Her breath caught. Suddenly the kitchen went as cold as if she'd left the front door wide-open. "Then who...?"

"Dana, you haven't eaten any of them, have you?"

"No." Who had left them if not Hud? She walked back over to the sink and was about to open the cabinet door to retrieve the box, when her eye was caught by something out the window.

Through the snow she saw a light flickering up on the hillside near the old homestead. Near the well.

She stepped over and shut off the kitchen light, plunging the kitchen into darkness. Back at the window she saw the light again. There was someone up there with a flashlight.

"Dana? Did you hear what I said? Don't eat any of the chocolates."

"Do you still have men up on the mountain at the well?" she asked.

"No, why?"

"There's someone up there with a flashlight."

She heard the rattle of keys on Hud's end of the line. "Stay where you are. I'll be right there."

Chapter Six

Dana hung up the phone and sneaked into the living room to turn out that light, as well. She stood for a moment in total darkness, waiting for her eyes to adjust.

Through the front window, the sky outside was light with falling snow. She listened for any sound and heard nothing but the tick of the mantel clock over the fireplace. After locking the front door, she crept back into the kitchen to the window again.

No light. Had she only imagined it? And now Hud was on his way over—

There it was. A faint golden flicker through the falling snow. The light disappeared again and she realized that the person must have stepped behind the old chimney.

She stared, waiting for the light to reappear and feeling foolish even with her pulse still hammering in her ears. If she hadn't been on the phone with Hud when she'd seen the light, she wouldn't have called for help.

She'd had trespassers on the ranch before. Usually they just moved along with a warning. A few needed to see the shotgun she kept by the door.

Obviously this was just some morbid person who'd heard about the body in the well and had sneaked in the back way to the ranch hoping to find…what? A souvenir?

She really wished she hadn't told Hud about the light. She could handle this herself. The light appeared again. The person moved back and forth, flashing the light around. Didn't the fool realize he could be seen from the house?

A thought struck her. What if it was a member of her family? She could just imagine her father or uncle up there looking around. Hud wasn't one to shoot first and ask questions later, but if he startled whoever was up there— Even if he didn't kill them, he'd at least think them guilty of something.

Or…what if it was the killer returning to the scene of the crime? What if he was looking for evidence he believed the marshal hadn't found?

The thought sent a chill running up her spine. She stepped away from the window and moved carefully to the front door again in the darkness. The roads were icy; she didn't know how long it would take Hud to get here.

She found the shotgun by the door, then moved to the locked cabinet, found the hidden key and opened the drawer to take out four shells. Cracking the double-barreled shotgun open, she slipped two shells in and snapped it closed again, clicking on the safety. Pocketing the other two shells, she returned to the kitchen.

No light again. She waited, thinking whoever it was had gone behind the chimney again. Or left. Or...

Her heart began to pound. Had he seen the lights go out in the ranch house and realized he'd been spotted? He could be headed for the house right now.

She'd never been afraid on the ranch. But then, she hadn't known there was a murdered woman's remains in the well.

The shotgun felt heavy in her hands as she started to move toward the back door, realizing too late that she'd failed to lock it. She heard the creak of a footfall on the back porch steps. Another creak. The knob on the back door started to turn.

She raised the shotgun.

"Dana?"

The shotgun sagged in her arms as the back door opened and she saw Hud's familiar outline in the doorway.

He froze at the sight of the shotgun.

"I didn't hear you drive up," she whispered, even though there wasn't any need to.

"I walked the last way so your visitor wouldn't hear my vehicle coming and run. When I didn't see any lights on, I circled the house and found the back door unlocked..." His voice broke as he stepped to her and she saw how afraid he'd been for her.

He took the shotgun from her and set it aside before cupping her shoulders in his large palms. She could feel his heat even through the thick gloves he wore and smell his scent mixed with the cold night air. It felt so natural, she almost stepped into his arms.

Instead he dropped his hands, leaving her aching for the feel of him against her, yearning for his warmth, his strength, even for the few seconds she would have allowed herself to enjoy it before she pushed him away.

She stepped past him to the window and stared up the hillside. There was only falling snow and darkness now. "I don't see the light now."

"I want you to stay here," Hud said. "Lock the door behind me."

"You aren't going up there alone?"

He smiled at her. "Does that mean you're not wishing me dead anymore?"

She flushed, realizing she *had* wished that. And fairly recently, too. But she hadn't meant it and now she was afraid that foolish wish might come true if he went up that hillside alone. "I'm serious. I don't want you going up there. I have a bad feeling about this."

He touched her cheek. Just a brush of his gloved fingertips across her skin. "I'll be all right. Is that thing loaded?" he asked, tilting his head toward the shotgun where he'd left it.

"It would be pretty useless if it weren't."

He grinned. "Good. Try not to shoot me when I come back." And with that, he was gone.

HUD MOVED STEALTHILY through the snowy night, keeping to the shadows of the house, then the barn and outbuildings as he made his way toward the pines along the mountainside.

Earlier, he'd caught glimpses of the light flickering through the falling snow as he'd run up the road toward the ranch house, his heart in his throat.

Now, the falling snow illuminated the night with an eerie cold glow. No light showed by the well, but he didn't think whoever it was had left. He hadn't heard a vehicle. More to the point, he didn't think whoever it was had finished what he'd come here to do.

His breath puffed out in a cloud around his face as he half ran through the fallen snow in the darkness of the pines.

He stopped at the edge of the trees in view of the old homestead. Snow fell silently around him in the freezing night air. He watched the play of shadows over the new snow. A quiet settled into his bones as he stilled his breathing to listen.

From this position, the dark shape of the chimney blocked his view of the well. He could see no light. No movement through the blur of snow.

The night felt colder up here, the sky darker. No breeze stirred the flakes as they tumbled down. He moved as soundlessly as possible, edging his way toward the dark chimney.

He hadn't gone far when he saw the impression of tracks in the new snow. He stopped, surprised to find that the footprints had formed a path back and forth along the edge of the old homestead's foundation as if the person had paced here. Making sure Dana saw the light and went to investigate? he thought with a start.

Again Hud listened and heard nothing but the occasional semi on the highway as it sped by into the night. The snow was falling harder, visibility only a few feet in front of him now.

If any place could be haunted, this would be the place, he thought. A gust of sudden wind whirled the snow around him and he felt a chill as if the woman from the well reached out to him, demanding justice.

He pulled his weapon and made his way toward the chimney, staying in the shadow it cast.

That's when he saw it. Something lying in the snow. A rope. As he moved closer, he saw that it was tied to the base of the old chimney and ran across the snow in the direction of the well.

Hud stared into the falling snow, but he couldn't see the top of the well at this distance. He took the flashlight from his coat pocket but didn't turn it on yet. Holding his gun in one hand and the flashlight in the other, he moved soundlessly along the length of rope toward the well opening.

DANA COULDN'T STAND STILL. She'd lost sight of Hud as well as the old homestead chimney as the storm worsened. Nor had she seen the light again.

She couldn't stand it any longer. She couldn't wait here for Hud.

She knew he'd be furious with her and had even tried to talk herself out of going up there as she pulled on her boots, hat, coat and gloves.

But ever since last night, she hadn't been able to shake the feeling that something horrible was going to happen. This morning when she'd found out about the bones in the well and that Hud was back in town, she'd thought that was the something horrible the premonition had tried to warn her about.

But as she picked up the shotgun and stepped out the back door into the darkness and snow, she was still plagued with the feeling that the worst was yet to come. And then there was her stupid birthday wish!

She took the road, feeling fairly safe that she couldn't be seen since she couldn't see her hand in front of her face through the snowfall. Sometimes she would catch a glimpse of the mountainside as a gust of wind whirled the snow away. But they were fleeting sightings and she was still too far away to be seen, so she kept moving.

The air was cold. It burned her throat, the snow getting in her eyes. She stared upward, straining to see the chimney, reminded of ranchers' stories about stringing clotheslines from the house to the barn so they didn't get lost in a blizzard.

She'd always prided herself on her sense of direction but she didn't chance it tonight. She could feel the rut of the road on the edge of her boot as she walked, the shotgun heavy in her hands, but at the same time reassuring.

As she neared the homestead, the wind swirled the snow around her and for an instant she saw the chimney dark against the white background. It quickly disappeared but not before she'd seen a figure crouched at the edge of the old homestead foundation.

HUD FOLLOWED THE ROPE to the well, stopping just short of the edge to listen. He edged closer to the hole. The rope dropped over the side into blackness. Still hearing nothing, he pointed the flashlight down into the well, snapped on the light and jerked back, startled.

He wasn't sure what he'd expected to see dangling from the rope. Possibly a person climbing down. Or trying to climb out.

He holstered his weapon, then kneeling, he shone the flashlight to get a better look. It was a doll, the rope looped like a noose around its neck.

What the hell?

He picked up the rope and pulled it until the doll was within a few feet of the top. Its face caught in the beam of his flashlight and he let out a gasp, all his breath rushing from him.

The doll had Dana's face.

He lost his grasp on the rope. The doll dropped back into the well. As he reached for the rope to stop its fall, he sensed rather than heard someone behind him.

Half turning, he caught movement as a large dark figure, the face in shadow, lunged at him, swinging one of the boards from the well.

A shotgun discharged close by as he tried to pull his weapon but wasn't quick enough. The board slammed into his shoulder, pitching him forward toward the gaping hole in the earth.

Hud dropped the flashlight and grabbed for the rope with both hands, hoping to break his fall if not stop it.

His gloved hands wrapped around the rope, but the weight of his falling body propelled him over the side and partway down into the cold darkness of the well. He banged against the well wall with his left shoulder and felt pain shoot up his arm. But he'd managed to catch himself.

He dangled from the rope, the doll hanging below him. He was breathing hard, his mind racing. Where the hell had the shotgun blast come from? He had a bad feeling he knew.

Bracing his feet against the wall, he managed to pull the gun from his holster, telling himself it couldn't have been Dana. He'd told her to stay in the ranch house.

He looked up, pointing the gun toward the well opening. He could wait for his attacker or climb out. Snowflakes spiraled down from a sky that seemed to shimmer above him iridescent white. He squinted, listening.

Another shotgun blast, this one closer.

Hud climbed as best he could without relinquishing his weapon. Only seconds had passed since the attack. But now time seemed to stand still.

Then in the distance he heard the growl of an engine turning over and, a moment later, another shadow fell over the top of the well above him.

He looked up through the falling snow and saw the most beautiful woman in the world lay down her shotgun and reach for him.

DANA'S HEART WAS IN HER THROAT as she looked down into the well and saw Hud hanging there.

He was alive, not broken at the bottom, but partway down a rope. That's all that registered at first. Then she saw him wince as he tried to use his left arm to holster his gun and pull himself up.

"You're hurt," she said, as if the pain were her own. "Here, let me help you."

She managed to get him up to the edge and drag him out into the snow. They lay sprawled for a few moments, both breathing hard from the exertion.

"Thanks," Hud said, turning his head to look over at her.

She nodded, more shaken now than she'd been when she'd looked over the edge of the well and had seen him hanging down there. Aftershock, she supposed. The time when you think about what could have happened. Realized how close it had been. She breathed in the night air as the sound of a vehicle engine died off until there was nothing but the sound of their labored breaths.

They were alone. Entirely alone, as if the rest of the world didn't exist.

Hud sat up and looked at her. He was favoring his left arm and she saw now that his jacket was ripped and dark with blood.

"Your arm... It's bleeding!"

He shook his head. "I'm fine. What about you?"

"Fine." She pushed herself up, her arms trembling with the effort.

His gaze met hers and he shook his head. Couldn't fool him.

She started to get to her feet, but he caught her sleeve, pulling her back to the ground beside him.

"Dana."

Her face crumpled as he encircled her with his good arm and pulled her tightly against him. His hug was fierce.

She buried her face into his chest, the snow falling around them.

When she pulled back, the kiss was as natural as sunrise. Soft, salty, sweet and tentative. And for a moment nothing mattered. Not the past, the pain, the betrayal. In that moment, she only recalled the love.

The snow stopped. Just like that. And the moment passed.

Dana pulled back, drowning in all the reasons she shouldn't love this man—wouldn't love this man. Not again.

HUD SAW THE CHANGE in her eyes. A quick cooling, as if her gaze had filmed over with ice. Just as her heart had five years ago.

She pulled away to pick up the shotgun from where she'd dropped it earlier. He watched her rise, keeping her back to him.

He got to his feet, searching the snow for his flashlight. His left arm ached from where he'd smacked it against one of the rocks embedded in the side of the well and split it open. The pain was nothing compared to what he'd seen in Dana's eyes.

Maybe he couldn't make up for what he'd done to her five years ago, but he sure as hell would find whoever had put the doll down the well. Whoever had tried to kill him tonight.

He heard a sound from Dana, part cry, part gasp, and realized that she'd found his flashlight and was now shining it down into the well.

Stepping to her side, he took the light from her, seeing the shock on her face as well as the recognition. "It's your doll?"

She nodded. "My father gave it to me for my sixth birthday. He thought it looked like me. How…" She met his gaze. "It was on a shelf in my old playroom along with the rest of the toys Mom saved for her—" Dana's voice broke "—grandchildren."

Mary Cardwell hadn't lived long enough to see any grandchildren be born. He could see what a huge hole losing her mother had left in Dana. Desperately he wanted to take her in his arms again. The need to protect her was so strong he felt sick with it.

He wanted to believe the doll had been put in the well as just a cruel prank meant to frighten her, but he feared it had been a trap. If Dana had come up here alone to investigate after seeing the light on the hillside, she would have been the one knocked into the well and there wouldn't have been anyone here with a shotgun to scare the would-be killer away. The thought was like a knife to his heart but as he stepped past her, pulled the doll the rest of the way up and removed the noose from its neck, he told himself that Dana needed a marshal now more than she needed a former lover.

"When was the last time you saw the doll?" he asked. The doll's hair was flattened with snow. Careful not to disturb any fingerprints that might be on it, he brushed the snow away, shocked again how much the face resembled Dana's.

"I don't know. The toys have been on the shelves in the playroom for so long I hardly notice. I don't go into that room much." Another catch in her voice. The playroom would only remind her of her mother, he thought. "I'd forgotten about the doll."

Well someone else hadn't.

She shivered as if she'd had the same thought.

"Let's get back to the house and out of this weather," he said.

The sky over their heads was a deep, cold midnight-blue as they walked back toward the ranch house. A few stars glittered like ice crystals as a sliver of moon peeked out from behind a cloud.

He made her wait on the porch, leaving her still armed with the reloaded shotgun while he searched the house. There was no sign that anyone had been there—not to drop off a box of chocolates or to steal a doll from a shelf in her old playroom.

"All clear," he said, opening the front door.

She stepped in, breaking down the shotgun and removing the shells. He watched her put the shotgun by the door, pocket the shells and turn toward him again. "Let me see your arm," she ordered.

He started to protest, but she was already helping him off with his jacket. His uniform shirt was also torn and bloodied, though the cut in his upper arm didn't look deep from what he could see.

"Come in here," she said, and he followed her to the kitchen where she motioned to a chair.

He sat, watching her as she brought out a first aid kit. He rolled his shirtsleeve up as she sat next to him, all her attention on the three-inch gash in his arm.

"You shouldn't have come up there, but I appreciate what you did," he said, his voice hoarse with emotion. "You quite possibly saved my life tonight."

"You should get stitches," she said as if she hadn't heard him. "Otherwise it will leave a scar."

"It won't be my first," he said.

She mugged a disapproving face and said, "This is going to sting." Her fingers gripped his upper arm.

He winced, the disinfectant burning into the cut.

"I warned you," she said, glancing up into his face. "Sure you don't want a ride to the emergency room?"

"Positive. A few butterfly bandages and I'll be as good as new."

She looked doubtful but went to work. He'd seen her doctor horses and cows before. He doubted doctoring him was any different for her. Except she liked the horses and cows better.

He couldn't help but think about the kiss. Man, how he had missed her.

"There, that should at least keep it from getting infected," she said, slamming the lid on her first aid kit and rising from the chair.

He touched her wrist and she met his gaze again. "Thanks."

She nodded and went to put the kit away.

He rose from the chair. "Mind if I take a look where that doll was kept?"

"I don't see how—" She stopped, then shrugged as if she didn't have the energy to argue.

He reminded himself that it was her birthday for a few more hours. What a lousy birthday.

He followed her up the stairs to what had once been her playroom. Mary had left it just as it had been when the kids were little.

The room was large with a table at its center surrounded by small chairs. There were books everywhere in the room and several huge toy boxes. The Cardwell kids had been blessed. One wall was filled with shelves and toys. There was a small tea set, stuffed animals, dolls and large trucks.

In the center, high on the wall, was a gaping hole where something had been removed. "That's where she has always been," Dana said, hugging herself as she stared at the empty spot on the shelf as if the realization that someone had to have come into the house and taken the doll had finally hit home.

"Who knew about the doll?" he asked.

She shook her head. "Only everyone who knew me. Angus probably showed it off at the bar for days before my sixth birthday. You know how he is."

Hud nodded. Anyone in the canyon could have known about the doll. "But how many people knew where you kept it?"

"Anyone who ever visited when we were kids knew about the playroom," she said.

"Or anyone in the family," he said, not liking what he was thinking.

"No one in my family would do this." Her face fell the instant the denial was out. It was a blood instinct to take up for your brothers and sister. But clearly, Dana wasn't entirely convinced her siblings were innocent of this.

She reached out for the doll he hadn't even realized he'd carried up the stairs.

He held it back. "Sorry, it's evidence. But I'll make sure you get it back. I want to take the chocolates you received, too."

She nodded, then turned and headed for the play-room doorway, moving like a sleepwalker. The day had obviously taken its toll on her. He looked around the room, then down at the doll in his gloved hand, thinking about Dana's siblings before following her to the kitchen.

She opened the cabinet doors under the sink and pulled out the trash can. Their gazes met. She'd thrown the candy away believing it had come from him. He never thought he'd be thankful for that.

"Mind if I take the plastic bag and all?" he asked.

"Be my guest."

"I could use another bag for the doll."

She got him one. He lowered the doll inside and tightened the drawstring, then pulled the other trash bag with the present in it from the container.

"I'll have the gift box dusted for prints and the candy tested," he said.

Her eyes widened. "You think the chocolates might have been...poisoned?"

He shrugged, the gesture hurting his arm.

The phone rang. She picked it up. He watched her face pale, her gaze darting to him, eyes suddenly huge.

He reached for the phone and she let him take it. But when he put the receiver to his ear, he heard only the dial tone. "Who was it?"

She shook her head. "Just a voice. A hoarse whisper. I didn't recognize it." She grabbed the back of the chair, her knuckles white.

"What did the caller say to you?" he asked, his stomach a hard knot.

"'It should have been you in the bottom of that well.'"

Hud checked caller ID and jotted down the number. He hit star 69. The phone rang and rang and finally was answered.

"Yeah?" said a young male voice.

"What number have I reached?" Hud asked.

What sounded like a kid read the number on the phone back to him. Hud could hear traffic on the street and what sounded like skateboarders nearby. A pay phone near the covered skate park in Bozeman?

"Did you see someone just make a call from that phone?" he asked the boy.

"Nope. No one was around when I heard it ringing. Gotta go." He hung up.

"I'm not leaving you alone in this house tonight," Hud said to Dana as he replaced the receiver. "Either you're coming with me or I'm staying here. What's it going to be?"

Chapter Seven

"You look like you've seen better days," Hilde said the next morning when Dana walked into the shop. "I heard you were at the Corral. So you decided to celebrate your birthday after all."

"Who told you I was at the Corral?" Dana hadn't meant her tone to sound so accusing.

Hilde lifted a brow. "Lanny. I ran into him this morning at the convenience store." She tilted her head toward the two coffee cups on the counter. "I brought you a latte. I thought you might need it."

How had Lanny known that she was at the Corral last night? she wondered as she placed her purse behind the counter. "Thanks for the coffee. I really could use it."

Hilde handed her one of the lattes. She held it in both hands, trying to soak up some of the heat. Lanny had also known that Hud was working late. With a shiver, she realized he'd been checking up on her. And Hud.

"Are you all right?" Hilde asked, looking concerned.

Dana shook her head. "I went by the Corral last night to talk to Dad, then Lanny took me to dinner for my birthday."

"Oh, you didn't mention you were going out with Lanny."

"I'd forgotten we had a date."

Hilde gave her a look she recognized only too well.

"It was our *last* date. I'd hoped we could be friends...."

"I hate to say this, but it's just as well," Hilde said.

Dana couldn't believe her ears.

Hilde raised her hands in surrender. "Hey, you were never going to fall in love with Lanny and we both know it."

Dana started to protest, but saved her breath. It was true.

"Maybe Hud coming back was a good thing."

Dana eyed her friend. "I beg your pardon?"

"I mean it. You need to resolve your issues with him."

"Resolve my issues? He slept with my sister when we were engaged!"

"Maybe."

"Maybe? There is no maybe about it. I caught them in bed together."

"Going at it?"

"No." Dana stepped back as if afraid she would ring her friend's neck.

"That's my point. You caught him in her bed, but you don't know what happened. If anything. Stacy has always been jealous of you. I wouldn't put anything past her."

"And what ready excuse do you have for Hud?" She held up her hands. "No, that's right, he was drunk and didn't know what he was doing."

"I know it sounds clichéd—"

"It sounds like what it is, a lie. Even if Stacy threw herself at him. Even if he was falling-down drunk—"

"Which would mean nothing happened."

Dana shook her head. "Hud wouldn't have left town the way he did if he'd been innocent."

"Did you ever give him a chance to explain?" Hilde asked.

"There was nothing that needed explaining. End of story." She turned and walked to the back of the store, surprised how close she was to tears. Again.

A few moments later she heard Hilde come up behind her. "Sorry."

Dana shook her head. "It's just seeing him again. It brings it all back."

"I know. I just hate to see you like this."

Dana turned, biting her lip and nodding as tears spilled out.

Hilde pulled her into a hug. "Maybe you're right. Maybe you should just kill the bastard. Maybe that's the only way you'll ever be free of him."

Hilde was joking but Dana knew that even in death she would still be haunted by Hud Savage. And after last night, she knew she didn't want him dead. Far from it.

She dried her tears and said, "Hud spent the night at my place last night."

Her friend's eyebrows shot up. "No way."

"He slept on the couch." She practically groaned at the memory of Hud's bare chest when she'd gone downstairs earlier. The quilt she'd given him down around his waist. His bare skin tanned from living in southern California. Muscled from working out.

"Dana, what's going on?"

She shook off the image and took a sip of the latte. It was wonderful. Just like her friend. "It's a long story." She filled Hilde in on what had happened last night. "That's why I look like I didn't get any sleep. I didn't." She shook her head. "Hilde, I can't understand why anyone would do those things."

"This voice on the phone, was it a man or a woman?"

"I don't know. It was obviously disguised." She shivered and took another drink of the coffee. It warmed her from her throat to her toes and she began to relax a little. In the daylight, she wasn't quite so scared. "You know what bothers me the most is that whoever put that doll in the well had to have taken it from the house. Just like whoever left the chocolates."

"Everyone knows you never lock your doors," Hilde said.

"I do now. I just can't understand why I'm being threatened. It has to have something to do with the woman whose remains were found in the well."

There was a soft knock on the door and both women turned to see their first customer—Kitty Randolph—looking at her watch.

"She's early but we're going to have to let her in, huh," Hilde said with a laugh. "You sure you're up to this today?"

"I would go crazy if I stayed home, believe me," Dana said as she started toward the door to unlock it and put up the open sign. "Good morning, Mrs. Randolph."

"Dana," the older woman said, then added, "Hilde," by way of greeting. Kitty Randolph was a petite gray-haired woman with a round cheery face and bright blue eyes.

"I was going to get back to you about the fundraiser," Dana said, instantly feeling guilty for not doing so.

Kitty patted her hand with a cool wrinkled one of her own. "Now, dear, don't you worry about that. I know something dreadful happened out at the ranch. You must tell me all about it while you match this color thread." She pulled the leg of a pair of blue slacks from a bag hooked on her arm. "I need to raise the hem. I hate it, but I'm shrinking and getting shorter every day." She chuckled. "Now what's this about a body being in the well?" she asked conspiratorially as she took Dana's arm and steered her toward the thread rack.

Dana picked up several spools of thread and held them to the pants in Kitty Randolph's bag.

She gave the elderly woman a short version of the discovery in the well.

"Any idea who she was?" Kitty asked.

Dana shook her head. "We might never know."

Kitty purchased her thread and left, promising to bring some of her wonderful chocolate chip cookies the next time she stopped by.

ARMED WITH PHOTOGRAPHS and information about the emerald ring found in the well, Hud drove to Bozeman first thing.

The jewelry store was one of those small, exclusive shops on Main Street. Hud tapped at the door just over the closed sign and a fit-looking, gray-haired man unlocked the door.

"Marshal Savage," the jeweler said, extending his hand. "You made good time."

Hud handed him the photographs and information taken from the ring.

"Oh, yes," Brad Andrews said as he examined the photos. "I remember this ring very well. A one-carat emerald set in a pear-shape with two half-carat diamonds on each side. A beautiful ring. Something you would notice a woman wearing." He looked up, still nodding.

"You can tell me who purchased the ring?" Hud asked.

"Of course. I remember this ring well. It was a twenty-fifth anniversary present. Judge Randolph purchased it for his wife, Kitty."

AS KITTY RANDOLPH LEFT Needles and Pins, several other ladies from the canyon entered the shop, also using the excuse of needing fabric or patterns or thread when they were really just interested in the latest goings-on at the Cardwell Ranch.

Dana could see how her day was going to go, but better here than being at the ranch. Especially alone.

At least that's what she thought until the bell over the door at Needles and Pins jangled and the last person she wanted to see came through the door.

Dana looked up from the fabric she was pricing and swore under her breath. Hilde had gone to the post office to mail a special fabric order so Dana was alone with no place to run as her sister, Stacy, stepped into the shop.

Stacy glanced around, looking almost afraid as she moved slowly to the counter and Dana.

Dana waited, wondering what her sister was doing here. Stacy didn't sew and, as far as Dana knew, had never been in the store before.

Stacy was two years her senior, with the same dark hair, the same dark eyes, and that was where the similarities ended. Stacy was willowy-thin, a true beauty and all girl. She'd never been a tomboy like Dana, just the opposite. Stacy had hated growing up on the ranch, wanting even from a very young age to live on a street in town that had sidewalks. "I never want to smell cow manure again," she'd said when she'd left home at eighteen. "And I will *never* marry a cowboy."

Dana always thought Stacy should have been more specific about the type of man she would marry. She'd married at nineteen, divorced at twenty-two, married again at twenty-four, divorced at twenty-nine, married again at thirty-two and divorced. None of them were cowboys.

"Hi, Dana," Stacy said quietly.

"Is there something I can help you with?" Dana asked in her store-owner tone.

Stacy flushed. "I...no...that is I don't want to buy anything." She clutched her purse, her fingers working the expensive leather. "I just wanted to talk to you."

Dana hadn't seen Stacy since their mother's funeral and they hadn't spoken then. Nor did she want to speak to her now. "I don't think we have anything to talk about."

"Jordan asked me to stop by," Stacy said, looking very uncomfortable.

Jordan. Perfect. "He didn't have the guts to do it himself?"

Stacy sighed. *"Dana."*

"What is it Jordan couldn't ask me?" She hated to think what it would be since her brother hadn't seemed to have any trouble making demands of her yesterday on the phone.

"He would like us all to get together and talk at the ranch this evening," Stacy said.

"About what?" As if she didn't know, but she wanted to hear Stacy say it. So far Jordan had been the one who'd spoken for both Clay and Stacy. Not that Dana doubted the three were in agreement. Especially when it came to money.

But Stacy ignored the question. "We're all going to be there at seven, even Clay," Stacy continued as if she'd memorized her spiel and just had to get the words out.

That was so like Jordan to not ask if it was convenient for Dana. She wanted to tell her sister that she was busy and that Jordan would have to have his family meeting somewhere else—and without her.

Stacy looked down at her purse. Her fingers were still working the leather nervously. As she slowly lifted her gaze, she said, "I was hoping you and I could talk sometime. I know now isn't good." Her eyes filled with tears and for a moment Dana thought her sister might cry.

The tears would have been wasted on Dana. "Now definitely isn't good." She'd gotten by for five years without talking to Stacy. Recently, she'd added her brothers to that list. Most of the time, she felt she could go the rest of her life without even seeing or hearing from them.

Stacy seemed to be searching her face. Of course, her sister would have heard Hud was back in town. For all Dana knew, Hud might even have tried to see Stacy. The thought curdled her stomach. She felt her skin heat.

"Mother came by to see me before she died," Stacy said abruptly.

It was the last thing Dana expected her sister to say. A lump instantly formed in her throat. "I don't want to hear this." But she didn't move.

"I promised her I would try to make things right between us," Stacy said, her voice breaking.

"And how would you do that?"

The bell over the door of the shop jangled. Kitty Randolph again. "This blue still isn't quite right," the older woman said, eyeing Stacy then Dana, her nose for news practically twitching.

"Let me see what else we have," Dana said, coming out from behind the counter.

"I hope I didn't interrupt anything," Mrs. Randolph said, stealing a look at Stacy who was still standing at the counter.

"No, Mrs. Randolph, your timing was perfect," Dana said, turning her back on her sister as she went to the thread display and began to look through the blues. She'd already picked the perfect shade for the slacks, but pretended to look again.

She suspected that Kitty had seen Stacy come into the shop and was only using the thread color as an excuse to see what was going on.

"How about this one, Mrs. Randolph?" Dana asked, holding up the thread the woman had already purchased.

"That looks more like it. But, please, call me Kitty. You remind me so much of your mother, dear."

Dana caught a glimpse of Stacy. Her face seemed even paler than before. She stumbled to the door and practically ran to her car. Unfortunately, Mrs. Randolph witnessed Stacy's hasty exit.

"Is your sister all right? She seems upset," Kitty said.

"Who wouldn't be upset after a body's been found in the family well," Dana said.

"Yes, who isn't upset about that," Kitty Randolph said, watching Stacy drive away.

Dana sighed, feeling guilty and then angry with herself for only upsetting her sister worse. But dammit, she had every reason to hate her sister.

She could practically hear her mother's voice filled with disapproval. "Families stick together. It isn't always easy. Everyone makes mistakes. Dana, you have to find forgiveness in your heart. If not for them, for yourself."

Well, Mom, now all three of them have banned together against me. So much for family.

And there was no getting out of the family meeting—or probably having to listen to her sister say she was sorry again. She just hoped Stacy didn't think that saying she was sorry over and over was going to fix things between them. Not even when hell froze over.

Sorry, Mom.

WHEN HUD RETURNED to his office, he had a message to call Coroner Rupert Milligan.

"Got an ID on your woman from the well," Rupert said, then cleared his throat. "It's Ginger Adams."

Hud had to sit down. He moved the files stacked on his chair and dropped into it.

"The doctor and dental records the crime lab sent down came back with a match on both dental and emergency room records," Rupert said.

Good God. Ginger Adams. In a flash, Hud saw her. A pretty redhead with a stunning body and the morals of an alley cat.

Hud closed his eyes as he kneaded his forehead. "You're sure it's Ginger?"

"It's a ringer," Rupert said, not sounding any happier about it than Hud. "I told you your suspect list could be as long as your arm, didn't I?"

"You were right about her being a waitress, too," Hud noted. Was that why Rupert had been acting strangely after coming out of the well yesterday? Because he'd suspected it was Ginger?

Ginger had waited tables at the Roadside Café, the place where locals hung out every morning, gossiping over coffee. Both of his deputies had been there just this morning. It was an old hangout for sheriff's department deputies, the local coroner—and the marshal.

Hud swore softly under his breath. "I thought she left town with some guy."

"Guess that's what we were supposed to think," Rupert said. "I gotta go. Calving season."

"I didn't realize you were still running cattle on your place."

"Helping a friend."

Hud had that feeling again that Rupert knew more about this case than he was saying. "Thanks for letting me know."

"Good luck with your investigation."

"Yeah." Hud didn't mention that he'd found the owner of the ring. He was still trying to figure out how it ended up in the same well as Ginger Adams—years later.

Holy hell. The woman had been rumored to have broken up more marriages in the canyon than Hud could shake a stick at. But there was at least one marriage that had definitely bit the dust because of Ginger—the marriage of Mary and Angus Cardwell.

Damn. As he hung up, he wondered how Dana was going to take the news. He started to dial her number. But he realized he couldn't tell her this over the phone.

Everyone knew the Cardwell marriage had been on the rocks, but Ginger, it seemed, had been the last straw. And now her body had turned up on the ranch. Add to that, someone was targeting Dana.

He picked up his hat, grabbing his new marshal jacket on the way out the door. His left arm still ached, the skin around the cut bruised, but Dana had done a good job of patching him up.

It was only a few blocks to Needles and Pins. He knew he had more than one reason for wanting to tell Dana the news in person. He wanted to see how she was doing. She'd left the ranch house so quickly this morning he hadn't even had a chance to talk to her.

Clearly she'd been avoiding him. Last night after he'd announced he wasn't leaving her alone, she'd started to argue, but then got him some bedding from the closet and pointed at the couch.

She'd gone to bed and he hadn't seen her again until this morning—and only for the length of time it had taken her to grab her coat and leave.

He was her least favorite person in the world, true enough. Except maybe for whoever had put that doll in the well—and called and threatened her afterward.

But he also wanted to see her reaction to the news that the body had been Ginger's. He was the marshal and he needed to find Ginger's killer as fast as possible so he could put a stop to whoever was threatening Dana. He couldn't help but believe the two incidents were connected somehow.

As he started to cross the street to Needles and Pins, Lanny Rankin stepped into his path.

Hud hadn't seen Lanny since he'd returned, but he'd known eventually he'd run into him. The canyon wasn't wide or long enough for their paths not to cross.

"Lanny," he said, seeing the set of the man's broad shoulders, the fire in his eyes. There'd been bad blood between the two of them as far back as Hud could remember. Lanny seemed to have a chip on his shoulder and it didn't help when Hud had started dating Dana.

Hud had known that Lanny would move in on Dana as soon as he was out of the picture. He'd seen the way Lanny had looked at Dana back in high school. In fact, Hud had wondered over the past five years if Lanny hadn't just been waiting for Hud to screw up so he would have his chance with Dana.

"Stay away from Dana," Lanny said. "I don't want her hurt again."

"Lanny, I don't want to get into this with you but my relationship with Dana is none of your business."

"Like hell," Lanny said, advancing on him. "I know you're the marshal now and you think you can hide behind that badge..."

"Go ahead. Take your best shot," Hud said, removing the marshal star from his coat and pocketing it.

Lanny's eyes narrowed as if he thought it was a trick. "You think you can get her back after everything you did to her?" He took a wide roundhouse swing.

The punch caught Hud on the left side of his jaw, a staggering blow that about took his feet out from under him.

He rubbed his jaw, nodding at Lanny who was breathing hard. "That's the end of it, Lanny." He reached into his pocket, took out the silver star and reattached it to his coat. "Dana's a grown woman with a mind of her own. She'll do whatever it is she wants to do no matter what either of us has to say about it."

Lanny rubbed his bruised knuckles.

Hud waited. He wanted this over with right here, right now.

"What the hell are you doing back here anyway?" Lanny asked, cradling his hand, which looked broken the way it was swelling up. "I would have thought you wouldn't have the nerve to show your face around here after what you did to her."

Hud ignored him. "Might want to have Doc Grady take a look at that hand, Lanny," he said, gingerly touching his jaw. Fortunately it wasn't broken but it hurt like hell. Lanny packed quite a wallop for a lawyer.

"She wasn't worth it," Lanny snarled, evening his gaze at him.

Hud knew Lanny was talking about Stacy now. And he couldn't have agreed more.

"She used you. She wanted a divorce in the worst way, but Emery didn't want to lose her. The old fool loved her for some crazy reason. But then she found a way to force his hand. After what happened between the two of you while he was out of town, he couldn't wait to get rid of her. Better than being the laughingstock of the canyon."

This was news to Hud. For years he'd tried to remember that night. He'd been told he got stinking drunk. He remembered wanting to. But after that, there was nothing in his memory banks until he woke up the next morning—in Dana's sister's bed.

After getting the anonymous note, Hud had come back to Montana convinced Stacy had somehow manipulated the incident just to get back at Dana. It was no secret that Stacy was jealous of her younger sister. He'd just never considered there might be more to it.

The thought gave him hope that he really had been set up. Maybe nothing had happened that night, just as he'd always wanted to believe. More to the point, maybe there was a way to prove it.

"You played right into Stacy's hands," Lanny said.

Hud nodded, saying nothing because he had no defense.

Lanny seemed to consider hitting him again, but must have changed his mind. "You hurt Dana again and that badge isn't going to stop me." With that, he turned and stormed off.

Hud watched Lanny go, hoping this really would be the end of it. But he couldn't get what Lanny had said about Stacy out of his head.

He needed to know what had happened that night. Nothing could have gotten him into Stacy's bed. At least nothing he remembered.

With a curse, he turned and saw Dana standing in the doorway of the sewing shop. From the expression on her face, she'd not only witnessed the ugly display between him and Lanny, she'd overheard it, as well.

DANA QUICKLY TURNED AND WENT back inside the shop, not wanting Hud to see her shock.

It was bad enough that everyone in the canyon knew about Hud and Stacy, but to hear Lanny talking about it... And could it be true that Stacy had done it—not to spite her—but to force Emery to give her a divorce?

She had to remind herself that whatever her sister's reasoning, Hud had gone along with it. So why was it getting harder and harder to call on that old anger?

She heard Hud come into the shop and tried to quit shaking. She was the one who should have left here and never come back, she thought. Instead it had been Hud who'd taken off, a sure sign of his guilt, everyone had said. While she'd stayed and faced all the wagging tongues.

"Dana?"

She turned to Hud, just as she'd faced the gossip that had swept through the canyon like wildfire.

"I'm sorry you heard that," he said.

"I'm sure you are. You'd much rather pretend it never happened."

"As far as I'm concerned, it didn't," he said.

"Let me guess," she said with a humorless laugh. "Your story is you don't remember anything."

"No, I don't."

All the anger of his betrayal burned fire-hot as if she'd just found out about it. "I really don't want to talk about this."

"We're going to have to at some point," he said.

She gave him a look that she hoped seared his skin. "I don't think so."

He shifted on his feet, then held up his hands in surrender. "That isn't why I came by." He glanced around the shop as if trying to lasso his emotions. In an instant, his expression had transformed. He was the marshal again. And she was... She saw something in his gaze. Something that warned her.

"We got an ID on the remains found in the well," he said. "Is there someplace we could sit down?"

She gripped the edge of the counter. If he thought she needed to sit, the news must be bad. But what could be worse than having a murdered woman's body found on your property?

Meeting Hud's gaze, she knew the answer at once—*having the marshal suspect that someone in your family killed her.*

Chapter Eight

Hud had expected more resistance but Dana led him to the back of the shop where there was a small kitchen with a table and chairs. The room smelled of chocolate.

"Hilde made some brownies," she said, then seemed to remember brownies were his favorite and something *she* used to make for him using a special recipe of her mother's.

"I'll pass on the brownies, but take some coffee," he said, spotting the coffeemaker and the full pot.

She poured them both some, her fingers trembling as she put down the mugs, and took a chair across from him. He watched her cup her mug in both hands, huddling over it as if it were a fire.

"So who is she?" Dana asked.

"Ginger Adams."

Dana paled as the name registered. She took a sip of the coffee, her hands shaking. "Ginger," she said on a breath, and closed her eyes.

He got up to get some sugar and cream for his coffee. He'd never really liked coffee. How could something that smelled so good taste so awful?

He took his time adding the cream and sugar before taking a sip. Her eyes were open again and she was watching him intently, almost as if she was trying to read his mind. If she could have, she'd know that all he could think about was how she used to feel in his arms.

"Have you talked to my father?" she asked.

"Not yet."

Her spine seemed to take on a core of steel. "It was over between them almost before it began. Ginger wasn't the reason my mother divorced Angus."

He said nothing, but wondered if she was defending her father. Or her mother. He'd known Mary Justice Cardwell. He couldn't imagine her killing anyone. But he knew everyone had the capability if pushed far enough.

And Mary was a crack shot. He doubted she would have only wounded Ginger Adams.

"I know it sounds like I'm defending him, but Ginger dumped him months before she supposedly left town with some other woman's husband," Dana said.

"Ginger dumped *him?*"

Dana seemed to realize her mistake. She'd just given her father a motive for murder. No man liked being dumped. Especially if he felt the woman had cost him his marriage. And then there was her father's old .38.

"Did Angus tell you Ginger was involved with a married man?" he asked.

She shrugged. "I can't remember where I heard that."

He studied her. Was there a grain of truth to Ginger being involved with another woman's husband? Maybe, given Ginger's propensity for married men. But he got the feeling Dana might be covering for someone.

"Any idea who the man was?" Hud asked.

Dana shook her head and looked down into her coffee mug. Whatever she was hiding would come out. Sooner or later, he thought.

In the meantime, he needed to talk to Kitty Randolph about her emerald ring.

"I NEED TO RUN AN ERRAND," Dana said the moment Hilde returned. "Can you watch the shop?"

"Are you all right? I saw Hud leaving as I was pulling in," her friend said.

"The woman in the well was Ginger Adams. That's what he came by to tell me."

Hilde frowned. "Ginger Adams? Not the Ginger who your dad…"

"Exactly," Dana said, pulling on her coat. "I'll be back."

Her father had a small place along the river on the way to Bozeman.

Dana took the narrow dirt road back into his cabin. His truck was parked out back. She pulled up next to it and got out. A squirrel chirped at her from a nearby towering evergreen; the air smelled of river and pine.

When she got no answer to her knock, she tried the door. Of course it opened. No one locked their doors around here. She stepped inside, struck by a wash of cool air, and saw that the door leading to the river was open. He must have gone fishing.

She walked out onto the deck, looked down the river and didn't see him. Turning, she spotted her father's gun cabinet and moved to it.

There were numerous rifles, several shotguns and a half-dozen different boxes of cartridges and shells. No .38 pistol, though.

"What are you looking for?"

Dana jumped at the sound of her father's voice behind her. She turned, surprised by his tone. "You startled me." She saw his expression just before it changed. Fear?

"You need to borrow a gun?" he asked, stepping past her to close the gun cabinet.

"I was looking for your .38."

He stared at her as if she'd spoken in a foreign language.

"The one you always kept locked in the cabinet."

He glanced at the gun cabinet. "I see you found the key."

"You've hidden it in the same place since I was nine." She waited. He seemed to be stalling. "The .38?"

"Why do you want the .38?"

"Are you going to tell me where it is or not?" she said, fear making a hard knot in her stomach.

"I don't know where it is. Wasn't it in the cabinet?"

Her father had never been a good liar. "Dad, are you telling me you don't have it?" She could well imagine what Hud was going to think about that.

"Why do you care? It wasn't like it was worth anything."

She shook her head. "Do I have to remind you that Ginger Adams was killed with a .38 and her remains were found on our property?"

All the color drained from his face in an instant. "Ginger?" He fumbled behind him, feeling for a chair and finding one, dropped into it. "Ginger?"

His shock was real. Also his surprise. He hadn't known it was Ginger in the well. "They're sure it's Ginger?" he asked, looking up at her.

She nodded. Had her father really cared about the woman? "Dad, you know Hud will want to see a .38 owned by someone with a connection to Ginger."

"Well, I don't know where it is. I guess I lost it."

"That's it?" Dana said, aghast, thinking what Hud would think.

Angus frowned and shrugged, but this time she saw something in his expression that made her wonder again what he was hiding from her. Was he protecting someone?

When she didn't say anything, he said, "I don't know what you want from me."

Her heart caught in her throat. She wanted him to tell her he was sorry for what he'd done. Splitting up their family. What she didn't want was for him to have killed Ginger Adams. Or be covering for someone else.

"I know that you and Jordan were both interested in Ginger," Dana said, the words coming hard.

His head jerked up in shock. "You knew?"

She'd found out quite by accident when she'd seen Jordan kissing a woman in the alley behind the building that would one day be Needles and Pins. Who could have missed Ginger Adams in that outfit she was wearing? The dress and shoes were bright red— just like her hair.

"It isn't what you think," her father said defensively. "I was never..." He waved a hand through the air. "You know. I can't speak for Jordan."

Like father like son. She shook her head in disgust as she sat in a chair next to him.

"Ginger was a nice young woman."

"You were *married*," she pointed out. "And Jordan was just a kid."

"Your mother and I were separated. I only lived at the ranch so you kids wouldn't know. Jordan was eighteen. I wouldn't say he was a kid."

"And you were forty."

He must have heard the accusation in her tone.

"And you're wondering what she could have seen in a forty-year-old man?" He laughed. "Sometimes you are too naive, sweetheart." He patted her head as he'd done when she was a child. "Dana," he said patiently, his eyes taking on a faraway look. "We can't change the past even if we'd like to." He got up from his chair, glancing at his watch. "I'm going to have a beer. I'm sure you won't join me but can I get you a cola?"

She stared at his back as he headed into the kitchen and after a moment she followed him. Sometimes he amazed her. Talk about naive.

"I don't think the past is going to stay buried, Dad, now that Ginger has turned up murdered and at the family ranch well. You and Jordan *are* suspects."

He glanced around the fridge door at her, a beer can in one hand, a cola in the other. He raised the cola can. She shook her head.

"If I were you I'd come up with a better story than you lost the .38," she continued, angry at him for thinking this would just pass. But that had been his attitude for as long as she'd known him. Just ignore the problem and it will fix itself—one way or another. That was her father.

Only this time, the problem wasn't going to go away, she feared. "Hud knows you had the gun. You used to let the two of us shoot it, remember?"

Her father nodded as he popped the top on his beer and took a drink. "Ahh-hh," he said, then smiled. "Of course I remember. I remember everything about those days, baby girl. Truthfully, honey? I don't know what happened to the gun. Or how long it's been gone. One day it just wasn't in the cabinet."

She was thankful that Hud didn't know about Ginger and Jordan. She'd never told Hud about the kiss in the alley she'd witnessed. And she doubted Jordan would be forthcoming about it.

She watched her father take a long drink and lick the foam from his lips. His gaze settled on her and a strange look came into his eyes. It was gentle and sad and almost regretful. "Sometimes you look so much like your mother."

HUD CALLED THE JUDGE'S number, a little surprised to learn that Kitty Randolph still lived in the same house she had shared with her husband. The same house where he'd been murdered five years before.

The maid answered. Mrs. Randolph had gone out to run a few errands and wasn't expected back until after lunch.

Lunch. Hud felt his stomach growl as he hung up. He hadn't eaten all day, but he knew a good place to get a blue plate special—and information at the same time.

Leroy Perkins had been a cook at the Roadside Café back when Ginger had been a waitress there. Now he owned the place, but hung out there most days keeping an eye on his investment.

Leroy was tall and thin and as stooped as a dogwood twig. His hair, what was left of it, was gray and buzz-cut short. He was drinking coffee at the end stool and apparently visiting with whoever stopped by and was willing to talk to him.

Hud slid onto the stool next to him.

"Get you a menu?" a young, blonde, ponytailed waitress asked him. She looked all of eighteen.

"I'll take the lunch special and a cola, thanks," Hud said.

She was back in a jiffy with a cola and a glass of ice along with the pot of coffee. She refilled Leroy's cup then went back into the kitchen to flirt with the young cook.

Leroy was shaking his head as he watched the cook. "Hard to find anyone who knows anything about the grill. There's a knack to cooking on a grill."

Hud was sure there was. "Leroy, I was wondering if you remember a waitress who used to work here back about twenty years ago."

"Twenty years? You must be kidding. I can barely remember what I had for breakfast."

"Her name was Ginger Adams."

Leroy let out a laugh. "Ginger? Well, hell yes. That cute little redhead? Who could forget *her?*" He frowned. "Why would you be asking about her? It's been…how many years? It was the year we got the new grill. Hell, that was seventeen years ago, the last time I saw her."

There was no avoiding it. Everyone in the canyon knew about the bones. Once he started asking about Ginger, any fool would put two and two together. "It was her bones that were found in the Cardwell Ranch well."

"No kiddin'." Leroy seemed genuinely surprised.

"You ever date her?" Hud asked.

The old cook let out a cackle. "She wasn't interested in some cook. Not that girl. She was looking for a husband—and one who could take care of her."

"Someone with money."

"Money. Position. Power. And it didn't matter how old he was, either," Leroy said grudgingly.

"Like Angus Cardwell."

Leroy nodded. "He was old enough to be her daddy, too. Guess she thought the Cardwell Ranch was his. Dropped him like a hot potato once she found out Mary Cardwell wasn't going to let loose of that land, though."

"Know who she dated after Angus?" Hud asked.

Leroy chuckled and took a sip of his coffee before he said, "Sure do. Went after the eldest son."

Hud couldn't hide his surprise. "Jordan?"

"Oh, yeah," Leroy said.

He wondered why he'd never heard about this. "You're sure? You said you could barely remember what you had for breakfast this morning...."

"I was here the night Jordan came by and the two had quite the row," Leroy said. "They didn't see me. I was just getting ready to bust the two of them up when he shoved her and she fell and broke her arm."

Hud felt a start. The broken wrist bone. "Jordan broke her arm?" he asked in surprise. "How, in this canyon, did something like that happen and not be public knowledge within hours?"

Leroy flushed. "Well, that could be because she was ready to file an assault charge against Jordan— until he promised to pay for all her expenses, including medical costs and lost wages."

"He paid you off, too," Hud guessed.

Leroy shrugged. "Cooking is the most underpaid profession there is."

So that's how Leroy started his nest egg to buy the café. "So what were Jordan and Ginger arguing about?"

"Seems he thought they had something going on," Leroy said. "She, however, had moved on to higher ground, so to speak."

The waitress returned and slid a huge plate covered with thick-sliced roast beef and a pile of real mashed potatoes covered with brown gravy and a side of green beans and a roll.

"So they didn't patch things up?" Hud asked in between bites.

Leroy laughed again. "Not a chance. Jordan tried to make it up to her, but she wasn't having any of it. Nope, Jordan was history after that."

"And this higher ground you spoke of?" Hud asked.

Leroy wrinkled his brow. "I just knew Ginger. She'd found herself someone else, probably someone with more potential than Jordan. Ginger didn't go five minutes without a man."

"But you don't know who he was?"

Leroy shook his head. "She took off time from the café while her arm healed. Didn't see much of her and then…she was just gone. I assumed she'd taken off with the guy. Her roommate said she packed up what she wanted of her things, even gave away her car, and left."

"Her roommate?"

"A bunch of girls bunked in one of those cheap cabins near the café but you know how it is, some last a day on the job, some a week. Very few last a summer. I barely remember the one roommate that Ginger used to hang with. A kind of plain girl, not a bad waitress, though."

"This friend never heard from her again?" Hud asked as he ate. The food was excellent.

Leroy shrugged. "None of us did, but we didn't think anything of it. Girls like Ginger come and go. The only thing they leave behind is broken hearts."

"Ginger have any family?" Hud asked.

"Doubt it or wouldn't someone have come looking for her? I got the feeling she might not have left home under the most congenial circumstances."

Hud had the same feeling. "Try to remember something more about this girl who befriended Ginger."

"She didn't work at the café long." He slapped his forehead. "I can almost think of her name. It was something odd."

"If you remember it, call me," Hud said, throwing down enough money to cover his meal and cola. "I wish you wouldn't mention this to anyone."

Leroy shook his head, but Hud could tell that the moment he left, Leroy would be spreading the word.

"Wait a minute," Leroy said. "There might be someone you could ask about Ginger." He seemed to hesitate. "Ginger used to flirt with him all the time when he came in." The cook's eyes narrowed. "You're probably not going to want to hear this…"

Hud let out a snort. "Let me guess. Marshal Brick Savage."

"Yeah, how'd you know?" Leroy asked, sounding surprised.

Hud smiled. "Because I know my father." He had another flash of memory of a woman in red. Only this time, he heard her laughter dying off down the street.

As Hud climbed into his patrol SUV, he turned south onto the highway and headed toward West Yellowstone and the lake house his father had bought on Hebgen Lake.

He couldn't put off talking to his father any longer.

Chapter Nine

"I wondered when I'd be seeing you," Brick Savage said when he answered the door. The former marshal shoved the door open wider and without another word, turned and walked back into the house.

Hud stepped in, closed the door, then followed his father to the back part of the house to the kitchen and small dining nook in front of a bank of windows.

He studied his father under the unkind glare of the fluorescent lights, surprised how much the elder Savage had aged. Hud remembered him as being much more imposing. Brick seemed shrunken, half the man he'd once been. Age hadn't been kind to him.

Brick opened the refrigerator door and took out two root beers. Hud watched him take down two tall glasses and fill each with ice cubes.

"You still drink root beer," Brick said. Not really a question. Root beer was about the only thing Hud had in common with his father, he thought as he took the filled glass.

"Sit down," Brick said.

Hud pulled up one of the chairs at the table, his gaze going to the window. Beyond it was a huge, flat, white expanse that Hud knew was the frozen snow-covered surface of Hebgen Lake. Not far to the southeast was Yellowstone Park.

He wondered why Brick had moved up here. For the solitude? For the fishing? Or had his father just wanted out of the canyon for some reason? Bad memories maybe.

"So what can I do for you?" Brick asked and took a long swig of his root beer.

Hud doubted his father was so out of touch that he hadn't heard about the woman's body that was found in the Cardwell Ranch well. In fact, Hud suspected the coroner had filled him in on every facet of the case.

"I'm investigating the murder of Ginger Adams," Hud said, watching his father's expression.

Nothing. Brick seemed to be waiting for more.

"Ginger Adams, a pretty redheaded waitress who worked at the Roadside Café seventeen years ago?" Hud said.

"What does that have to do with me?" Brick asked, sounding baffled.

"You knew her."

Brick shrugged. "I'm sorry, but I don't remember her. I don't remember most of them."

Hud cursed under his breath. "Well, I remember. I keep seeing Ginger in a slinky red dress and red high heels. And for some reason, I keep seeing you with her."

"Could have been me," he admitted congenially. "That was how many years ago?"

"Seventeen according to Leroy at the café."

Brick nodded. "The year your mother died. Oh, yeah, it could have been me." Brick looked down at his half-empty glass of root beer.

Hud rubbed a hand over his face, feeling the old anger toward his father. "You broke her heart, you know."

"I broke your mother's heart long before she got sick," his father said. "I was your mother's number one disappointment." He looked up at Hud. "Isn't that what she always told you?"

"She loved you."

Brick laughed. "Maybe. At one time. You won't believe this, but your mother was the only woman I ever loved."

"You had an odd way of showing it."

"You disappoint a woman enough times and you quit trying not to. But you didn't drive all this way to talk about this, did you?"

Hud cleared his throat. There was no point getting into the past. He couldn't change it. He couldn't change his father and his mother was dead. He dropped the case file on the table between them. "I need to ask you some questions about Judge Raymond Randolph's killing."

Something showed in Brick's face. "Is there something new in that case?"

Hud thought he heard a slight waver in his father's voice, but then he might have imagined it.

"If you read my report, you know as much as I do about the case," Brick said, glancing down at the file but not reaching for it.

"I've read the file," Hud said.

"Then you know what happened that night," Brick said. "I took the call from a neighbor who heard gunshots at the judge's house. I tried to reach you and couldn't, so I went instead."

Hud knew Brick would remind him of that.

"According to your report, you saw the Kirk brothers coming out of the judge's house and gave chase."

His father eyed him, no doubt bristling at the use of his exact words. "That's exactly what happened."

"The vehicle, an older model car, was being driven by one of the Kirk brothers, Ty. Mason was with him in the passenger seat."

"That's right," Brick said. "I chased them down the canyon almost to Gallatin Gateway."

"Almost. According to your report, Ty lost control of the car at the 35-miles-per-hour curve just before the bridge. Both men were killed. Later you reported that several items from the judge's house were found in the car. The conclusion was that the judge had come home early, caught the Kirk brothers in the act of burglarizing the house and was fatally injured when one of the brothers panicked and shot him with a .38-caliber pistol. The judge's wife, Kitty, was out of town. The boys ran, you chased them, they both died in the car wreck."

"You have a problem with my report?"

Hud rubbed his bruised jaw, never taking his eyes off his father. "It's just a little too cut-and-dried, because now, something stolen from the judge's house that night has turned up in the Cardwell Ranch well—along with the remains of Ginger Adams."

The older man's shock was real. Rupert couldn't have told him about the owner of the ring because the coroner hadn't known.

"If Ginger was killed the night she allegedly left town seventeen years ago and the robbery was only five years ago, then how did Kitty Randolph's ring end up in the well?"

Brick shook his head. "I'm supposed to know?"

"You know what bothers me about this case?" Hud said. "Nowhere in the original report does it say that there was any item found on the brothers that connected them to the robbery and murder of the judge."

"Doesn't it say that a pair of gold cuff links and a pocket watch were found in the glove box of the car?" Brick said.

Hud nodded. "That information was added later." Both items were small and could easily have been put in the car—after the accident. "You know what else is missing? The .38. What happened to the gun? And where did they get a gun that had been used in a murder years before—back when both brothers were barely out of diapers?"

"They could have found the gun. Then after using it, threw it in the river during the chase," Brick said with a shrug.

"Maybe..." Hud agreed "...but I'm sure you had deputies looking for the gun, right?" His father nodded, a muscle bunching in his jaw. "Never found, right?" Again his father nodded. "Leaves a lot of questions since both Kirk boys are dead and the gun is missing."

"Life is like that sometimes," Brick said. "You don't always find the answers."

"Weren't drugs found in their car after the accident?"

His father nodded slowly and picked up his glass to take a drink.

"If the Kirks had gotten caught with drugs again wouldn't they both have been sent to Deer Lodge? It would have been the third offense for both of them. They would have been looking at some hard time."

"Rather a moot point since they were both killed," Brick said.

"My point exactly. Isn't it possible that the drugs were the reason they ran that night and not that they'd just burglarized Judge Randolph's house and murdered him?"

Brick put down his glass a little too hard. "Son, what exactly are you accusing me of?"

What was he accusing his father of? "I'm not sure justice was done that night."

"Justice?" His father let out a laugh. "For years I chased down the bad guys and did my best to get them taken off the street. The Kirk brothers are just one example. Those boys should have been locked up. Instead, because of overcrowding in corrections, they got probation for the first offense and saw very little jail time for the second. The law put them back on the street and they ended up killing Judge Randolph. I saw them come running out of his house, no matter what you believe."

"You sure you didn't see a chance to get Ty and Mason Kirk off the streets for good?"

Brick shook his head sadly. "You're wrong, but let me ask you this. This murder you got on your hands, what if you find out who killed her but you can't prove it? You think you'll be able to pass that killer on the street every day knowing he did it and him thinking he got away with it?"

"We aren't talking about the Kirk brothers now, are we."

Brick took a drink of his root beer. "Just hypothetical, son."

"Right before he was killed five years ago, Judge Randolph was threatening to have you fired from your job," Hud said. "He seemed to think you'd been playing fast and loose with your position of power."

"Five years ago, I was getting ready to retire, you know that. What would I care if the judge got me fired?"

"If you'd gotten fired, you would have lost your pension," Hud said.

Brick laughed. "And you think I'd kill someone for that measly amount of money?" He shook his head still smiling as if he thought this was a joke.

"Maybe the judge had something on you that would have sent you to jail."

He laughed again. "Hell, you would have gotten the marshal job if I had gone to jail."

Hud knew now that he'd only taken the deputy job to show his father. Brick had been dead set against it and done everything he could to keep Hud out of the department. But his father was right about one thing, Hud would have been up for marshal in the canyon.

"Tell me something," Hud said. "Why were you so dead set against me being a deputy?"

"I knew what kind of life it was. I didn't want that for you. Maybe I especially didn't want it for Dana. I know how much your mama hated me being in law enforcement. Isn't it possible that I was trying to protect you?"

It was Hud's turn to laugh. "I think you were protecting yourself. You knew I'd be watching you like a hawk. I think you were worried I'd find out what the judge had on you."

"I hate to burst your bubble, but the judge had nothing on me. In fact, he was about to be removed from the bench," Brick said. "He had Alzheimer's. He was losing his mind. His allegations against me were just part of his irrational behavior."

Hud stared at his father. Could that possibly be true?

Brick picked up their empty glasses and took them to the sink. "I'll admit I've made my share of mistakes," he said, his back to Hud. "I thought you only took the deputy job to prove something to me. I didn't want you following in my footsteps for the wrong reasons."

Hud *had* taken the job for all the wrong reasons. But law enforcement must have been in his blood. It had turned out to be the right career for him.

His father turned to look back at him. "Did you know your mother wanted me to go into business with her father? She married beneath her. We both knew it. Everyone told her she could do better than me. She just wouldn't listen. She thought I'd change my mind once you were born." He turned back to the sink.

Hud stared at his father's back, thinking about the things his mother used to say about Brick. She'd been angry at her husband as far back as Hud could remember. Now he wondered if a lot of that anger and resentment hadn't stemmed from Brick not going to work for her father. Had she been embarrassed being married to a small-town marshal?

Brick shut off the water and dried his hands. "I know you think I killed your mother, not cancer. Maybe I did. Maybe her disappointment in me caused the cancer." He stood against the sink, looking small and insubstantial. "I was sorry to hear about you and Dana. I always thought you made a nice couple."

Hud picked up the Judge Randolph case file from the kitchen table. He'd thought coming up here to see his father would be an end to all his questions. Now he had even more questions. "I'm going to solve these murders."

"I don't doubt you will," Brick said. "You were always a damned good deputy. I thought after what happened five years ago, you'd be soured on the profession. You know I had to suspend you the night the judge was killed just like I would have had to any deputy who blew his shift. I couldn't protect you because you were my son."

He studied his father. "It must have been a shock to you then to hear that I'm the temporary marshal until they can advertise the job."

Brick smiled but said nothing.

Hud started toward the door, stopped and turned. "You didn't seem surprised."

"About what?"

"About the ring that was found in the well with Ginger's remains." He studied his father. "Because you already knew, didn't you?"

"Good luck with your investigation, son."

DANA RETURNED TO THE SHOP to find it packed with customers. She met Hilde's eye as she came in the door and saw her friend wink mischievously. They hadn't even had this much business during the rush before Christmas—and January was when most businesses felt a slump.

But here it was January and the shop was full of women. It didn't take a genius to figure out what was up.

Hilde cut fabric while Dana rang up purchases and answered questions relating to the bones found in the ranch well and a rumor that was circulating that the bones belonged to Ginger Adams.

Dana fudged a little. "Ginger Adams? *Really?*"

The afternoon whizzed by. Dana tried not to watch the door, afraid Hud would pay her another visit. But by closing, he hadn't shown and she breathed a sigh of relief when Hilde offered to take the deposit to the bank and let Dana finish closing up.

"Can you believe this?" Hilde said, hefting the deposit bag. She grimaced. "Sorry. I do feel bad making money at your expense. And Ginger's."

"S'all right," Dana said, laughing. "It's a windfall for the store. At least something good is coming out of it."

Hilde left and Dana straightened the counter before going to lock up. As she put the closed sign up on the front door, she was surprised how dark it was outside. It got dark early this time of year. Plus it had snowed off and on most of the day, the clouds low, the day gloomy. There was no traffic on the street and only a few lights glowed at some of the businesses still open this time of the afternoon.

As she looked out, a movement caught her eye. She stared across the street into the shadowy darkness at the edge of the building. Had she only imagined it or was someone standing there looking in her direction?

She stepped to the side to make sure the light in the back wasn't silhouetting her and waited, unable to shake the feeling that someone had been watching her as intently as she had been staring across the street at them.

Lanny? He'd spied on her last night and on Hud, as well. But surely he wasn't still doing it.

Or Hud? That would be just like him to keep an eye on her.

Another thought struck her. Could it be the person who had left the chocolates for her? The same person who'd taken her doll and put it in the well last night? She shivered, remembering the voice on the phone. Just a prank call, she kept telling herself.

A sick, morbid cruel prank. Was it possible that's all the chocolates and the doll in the well were meant to be? The prankster had just been having fun at Dana's expense but then she'd had to go and call the marshal and things got out of hand?

That's what she wanted to believe as she stepped to the window again and looked out. Nothing moved. The lights of a car came down the winding street, blinding her for a moment as it swept past.

In that instant as the car passed, the headlights illuminated the building across the street.

No one was there.

She'd been so sure she'd seen a person watching her.

On impulse, she reopened the front door and ran across the street without her coat, leaving the shop door wide-open.

It would only take a second to find out if she was losing her mind or not.

THE MOMENT HUD HIT the highway, he called Judge Raymond Randolph's widow to see if Kitty had returned home. It would have been better to stop by and see her, but she lived at the other end of the canyon. He'd spent longer at his father's than he'd meant to. Now he was running late. He wouldn't be able to drive down to see her and still get back to Needles and Pins before Dana left for the night, and he was worried about Dana.

But he needed to know if anything his father had told him was the truth.

"Hello?" Kitty's voice was small but strong.

"Mrs. Randolph?" He remembered Katherine "Kitty" Randolph as being tiny and gray with smooth pink skin and twinkling blue eyes. She baked the best chocolate chip cookies and always brought them to the church bake sales.

"Yes?"

"My name is Hudson Savage. You probably don't remember me."

"Hud," she said, her tone more cheerful. "Of course I remember you. You and your mother used to sit near me in church. Your mother baked the most wonderful pies. I think her apple pie was my favorite. I couldn't help myself. I always purchased a slice at every sale. For a good cause, I'd tell myself." She let out a soft chuckle, then seemed to sober. "I remember your mother fondly. You must miss her terribly."

He'd forgotten about his mother's pies. Her crust would melt in your mouth. Pies were her one pride.

He cleared his throat. "Yes. I hate to bother you this evening but I'm the new interim marshal in Gallatin Canyon and I'm involved in an investigation." He hesitated, unsure how to proceed.

"That woman's bones that were found in the well on the Cardwell Ranch," Kitty Randolph said. "Yes, I heard about it. How horrible. But I don't see what I—"

"The woman is believed to have been killed with the same gun that killed your husband."

Kitty let out a small gasp and Hud wished he'd been more tactful. He should have done this in person. He should have waited. But since he hadn't, he dove right in.

"I need some information about the last few months the judge was alive." He took a breath. "Did he have Alzheimer's and was he about to be asked to step down from the bench?"

Silence, then a shaky croak. "Yes, I'm afraid so."

Hud let out a breath. "I'm sorry. That must have been very difficult for you. I understand his behavior was sometimes irrational."

"Yes," she repeated. "This is about your father, isn't it?"

Behind the twinkling blue eyes, Kitty had always shown a sharp intelligence.

"Yes. Mrs. Randolph, do you know what the judge had against my father?"

"No, I never understood his animosity toward Marshal Savage," she said, sounding sad. "But the judge was a hard man. Much like your father. And who knows how much of it was just my husband's illness."

"Were there any papers missing after the judge's death?" Hud asked.

"You mean, some evidence my husband might have had on your father?"

That was exactly what he meant.

"No. I doubt any existed." She sounded tired suddenly.

"I know it's late. I just have one more question. In the burglary report, you didn't mention a ring."

"No," she said, sounding tentative.

"Well, Mrs. Randolph, an emerald ring was found."

Another gasp. "You found my ring?"

"Yes, I'm afraid it's being held as evidence."

"I don't understand."

He cleared his throat again. "The ring was found in the well with the remains of Ginger Adams."

Another gasp, this one more audible than the first. For a moment he thought she might have dropped the phone. Or even fainted. "Mrs. Randolph?"

"I had to sit down," she said. "I don't understand. How is that possible?"

"I was hoping you might have some idea," Hud said.

"This is very upsetting."

"I'm sorry to have to give you the news on the telephone," he said as he drove. "Do you have any idea how long the ring has been missing?"

"No, I didn't look for it for months after the judge's death and when I did, I realized it was missing. I thought about calling the marshal and letting him know, but your father had retired by then and I just assumed it had been lost when those young men wrecked their vehicle in the river. I never thought I'd see it again." She sounded like she might be crying. "The judge had it made for me in honor of our twenty-fifth wedding anniversary."

"I understand it's an expensive piece of jewelry," Hud said.

"The only piece of real jewelry the judge ever bought me. When we married, he couldn't afford a diamond." Her voice broke.

Hud frowned. "Wouldn't you have kept a piece of expensive jewelry like that in a safe or a safe-deposit box at the bank?"

Ahead he could see the lights of Big Sky. The Kirk brothers hadn't found the safe. Nor would they have known how to open it if they had.

"I thought it was in the safe," Kitty said. "Obviously, I had taken it out to wear it and forgot to put it back. The judge probably saw it and put it in the jewelry box with his cuff links and his father's old pocket watch."

But it didn't explain how the ring ended up in the well. "I'll see what I can do about getting the ring returned to you as soon as possible," Hud told her.

"Thank you. I can't tell you what your call has meant to me. Good night, Hud."

He disconnected as he turned off and drove up to Big Sky's lower meadow. As he started to turn down the street to Needles and Pins, a car whipped out of the marshal's office parking lot, tossing up gravel.

The driver spotted him and threw on his brakes. The vehicle's door flew open and Jordan Cardwell jumped out.

"I want to talk to you, Savage," he said, storming over to the SUV.

"How about that," Hud said. "I want to talk to you, too, Jordan. Now just isn't a great time."

"Too bad," Jordan said. "I want to know what the hell is going on out at the ranch."

DANA STOPPED AT THE EDGE of the building across the street from the fabric shop, waiting for her eyes to adjust to the darkness. The air was cold, the shadows dark and deep along the side of the building.

She saw that the sidewalk across the front had been shoveled but there was new snow along the side of the closed office building. She stepped into the dark shadows, almost convinced she'd only imagined a figure standing here. What fool would stand in all that snow just to—

She saw the fresh tracks. Her heart lodged in her throat. The snow was tramped where someone had stood. Waiting. She glanced behind her and saw that from this spot, the person had a clear view of the shop.

Behind the spot where the snow was trampled was a set of tracks that came up the narrow passage alongside the building. Another set returned to the alley.

For one wild moment she thought about following them. She even placed her boot into one track. The shoe size was larger than her own, but the edges caved in after each step the person had taken so it was impossible to gauge a true size of the print.

She shivered as she looked toward the dark alley, seeing nothing but the tracks. Only a fool would follow them. Whoever had been standing here watching the shop only minutes ago might not be gone, she told herself. He'd seen her look out the window. Maybe that's what he'd been waiting for. For her to see him. And follow him?

But why? It made no sense. It was as if someone was just trying to scare her. Unless the chocolates were filled with poison. And she was the one who was supposed to have been knocked down into the well last night.

Just like Ginger Adams had been?

Just like her caller had said.

She hugged herself against the bone-deep cold of her thoughts as she turned and ran back across the street. Halfway across she noticed the shop door. She'd left it wide-open, but now it was closed. The wind must have blown it shut.

But as she opened it and stepped tentatively inside, she tried to remember feeling even the slightest breeze while she was across the street—and couldn't.

As she stood in the darkened shop, she realized someone could have slipped in while she was gone. It had been stupid to run out like that and leave the door wide-open. Worse, she realized, she hadn't locked the back door of the shop because she was planning to go out that way.

She held her breath, listening for a sound. The shop was deathly quiet. The small light still burned in the back room, casting a swath of pale gold over the pine floor.

Her teeth began to chatter. Glancing out into the street, she saw only darkness. Again she looked toward the back of the shop where she'd left her purse, her cell phone, her car keys.

There's no one in here. No one hiding behind the rows of fabric.

Even if the person who'd been across the street *had* been watching her, what were the chances he had circled around and come into the shop when she wasn't watching and was now waiting for her?

She started to take a step toward the back of the shop.

Silent and huge, a shadow loomed up from the darkness and came out of the stacks of fabric. A large silhouette against the light in the back.

She screamed as he reached for her. She shot an elbow out, stumbling backward into one of the fabric rows.

"Dana. It's me."

But it was too late. She'd already driven her elbow into his ribs and sent a kick to his more private parts. Fortunately for Hud, the kick missed its mark.

She heard him let out a curse followed by her name again. "It's me. Hud."

As if she hadn't already recognized his voice.

A flashlight beam illuminated a spot on the floor at their feet.

"What are you doing?" she demanded. "You scared the life out of me."

He rubbed his thigh where her boot had made contact and eyed her suspiciously.

"What are you doing here anyway?" she asked.

"I came in through the back. The door was unlocked. When I saw the front door standing open, I was afraid something had happened to you." He turned on the light and she saw how worried he looked.

She swallowed back a retort. "That wasn't you watching from across the street then?"

"There was someone watching you from across the street?" He was already headed for the door.

"Whoever it was is gone," she called after him.

"Stay in the shop. Lock the doors," he called over his shoulder without looking back as he crossed the street.

Hurriedly, she locked the back door, then the front, and from the window watched the flicker of his flashlight beam moving across the snow.

She saw him stop at the spot she'd discovered between the buildings, no doubt following the footprints she'd seen in the snow.

She waited, hating that Hud had acted so quickly on something that was probably innocent. Maybe it had been someone waiting for a friend who didn't show. Maybe the whole thing had nothing to do with her. Hud taking it seriously only made her more anxious.

Was she really in danger?

What scared her was that he seemed to think so.

He came back across the street and she unlocked the door to let him in. He closed the door behind him, locking it.

"Nothing, right?" she asked hopefully.

"I don't want you going back to the ranch by yourself."

She'd let him stay last night because she'd been as scared for him as for herself. But she hadn't been able to sleep knowing he was downstairs, so close.

She shook her head. "I won't be driven out of my home."

"Then I'm staying with you."

"No. That is, I won't be alone tonight. We're having a family meeting. I'll get Clay or Jordan to stay with me. I'll be fine. Anyway, no one has any reason to harm me," she said, trying to convince herself as well as him. "I didn't put Ginger Adams in that well."

"But someone in your family might have. And quite frankly, having one of the suspects staying in the house with you might not be the best plan." His gaze softened. "Dana, why didn't you tell me that Jordan is forcing you to sell the ranch?"

Dana stared at Hud. "Jordan told you that?"

"In so many words, yes. Is there really a will?"

"I don't know." She sighed. His gaze filled with such tenderness it was like a physical pain for her. "I thought so at first. Mom told me she wrote up a draft and signed and dated it. Unfortunately, I can't find it and since she never got a copy to her lawyer before her death... Jordan is convinced I made up the whole story about Mother's new will."

"So, the ranch goes to all her heirs," Hud said, sympathy in his voice.

"Yes, and they have decided they want the money, which means I have no choice but to sell," Dana said. "I'm fighting to hang on to the house and a little land. That is what has been holding things up."

"Dana, I am so sorry."

She turned away. "Please, I hate talking about this." She remembered something he'd said and frowned as she turned to face him again. "You don't really think someone in my family had anything to do with Ginger's death, do you?"

He had on his cop face again, giving nothing away. "Anyone who had contact with Ginger or access to the ranch is a suspect."

She let out a surprised breath. "So I'm a suspect, too."

He sighed. "Dana, I've been thinking about what happened at the ranch last night. Is there anyone who might want to hurt you?"

She laughed. "What were we just talking about? I'm holding up the sale of the ranch and my three siblings are all chomping at the bit to get their hands on the money from the property."

"You seriously believe one of them would try to hurt you?" he asked.

"You know them." Her gaze locked with his. "There is little they wouldn't do to hurt me. Have done to hurt me."

"I have to ask you this," he said. "Last night, did you see the person who attacked me?"

"Why are you asking me this now?"

"I need to know if the reason you fired that shotgun in the air last night was to help someone in your family get away."

She stared at him, anger rising in her. "How can you ask me that?"

"Dana—" He reached for her, but she stepped back.

"You broke my heart." The words were out, surprising her as much as they did him. They had nothing to do with what he'd accused her of. They were also words she never thought she would admit to him of all people.

"I'll never forgive myself for letting it happen."

"Good." She started to step past him, but he grabbed her wrist.

"I made the worst mistake of my life that night," he said quickly.

Wouldn't Stacy love to hear that?

"You were everything to me."

"Apparently not," she snapped, trying to pull free. But his grip was firm, his fingers warm and strong.

"I truly don't remember that night," he said, his voice low and filled with emotion. "The last thing I remember is having a drink at the bar—"

"I told you I don't want to talk about this," she said.

"You have never let me tell you what happened. At least what I remember."

"Finding you in my sister's bed was sufficient enough."

"Dana, I've thought about this for five years, thought of little else. One drink and then nothing. I remember *nothing*."

"Well, that's your story, isn't it? That lets you off the hook."

"Dammit, why do you think I came back? Because of you and to prove that nothing happened that night."

"I thought you don't remember."

"I don't. I couldn't be sure before but I got a note from someone in the canyon that said I was set up that night."

"Who?"

"It was anonymous, but, Dana, I believe I *was* set up. Otherwise, why can't I remember that night? What I've never been able to understand is why? All I knew for sure is that your sister had to be in on it. But after what Lanny said earlier... Your sister couldn't have acted alone. Someone helped her."

Dana didn't move. Didn't breathe. All she could do was stare at him, remembering what she'd overheard Lanny tell him. That Stacy had used Hud to force Emery into giving her a divorce. Emery had been thirty years Stacy's senior, an older man with money. That was until he hooked up with Stacy. Stacy got her divorce five years ago—and took half of Emery's assets and his home.

What if Stacy had done it not to hurt Dana but for her own selfish reasons?

"Dana, if I was as drunk as everyone at the bar said I was, then believe me, I didn't sleep with your sister," Hud said. "I swear to you. I had one drink at the bar, then the rest of the night is a total blank. What does that sound like to you?"

That he'd been drugged.

"How was it that you showed up at Stacy's house so early the next morning?" he asked.

She swallowed, remembering the strange phone call, the strange voice. *Do you know where your fiancé is? I do. In your sister's bed.* She'd just thought it was some canyon busybody and told Hud about the call.

"I figured it had to be something like that. Which only makes me more convinced Stacy was behind it—and she wasn't working alone. My guess is that Stacy got some man to help her. I don't know why or how they did it, but I'm going to find out." He let go of her wrist, the look in his eyes a painful reminder of the love they'd once shared. "I've never wanted anyone but you. And I'm going to prove it to you."

She stood just looking at him, afraid of what she might say at that moment. Even more afraid of what she might do. They were so close that she could smell the faint hint of his aftershave and the raw maleness of him. She wanted desperately to believe him.

Her gaze went to his lips. The memory of his mouth on hers was like a stabbing pain. All she wanted was for him to take her in his arms, to kiss her again, to make her forget everything that had happened.

He reached for her, his large palm cupping her cheek, as he pulled her to him. She felt her body start to lean toward him like metal to magnet and the next thing she knew their lips brushed then locked.

She clutched the front of his jacket, balling up the fabric in her fists as his arms came around her. His tongue touched hers and desire shot through her. She moaned as he deepened the kiss, so lost in his mouth that she didn't even hear the first ring.

His cell phone rang again, shattering the silence, shattering the moment. She pulled back. He looked at her as if the last thing he wanted to be at that moment was marshal. The phone rang again. Slowly, he withdrew his arms and checked caller ID.

"I have to take this," he said, sounding as disappointed as she felt.

She stepped away from him, taking a deep breath and letting it out slowly. What had she done? She shook her head at how easily she had weakened. What was wrong with her? How could she forget the pain Hud had caused her?

Did she really believe he'd been set up? That nothing had happened that night except someone trying to drive them apart?

"Sheriff's department business. Sorry," he said behind her.

She touched her tongue to her upper lip, then turned to face him and nodded. "I need to get home, too. Wouldn't want to miss the family meeting Jordan's scheduled at the ranch tonight."

Hud swore. "Be careful. I'll call you later. I don't want you staying at the ranch house, especially with Jordan there. He told me just a while ago that he doesn't remember Ginger Adams nor did he have any contact with her." Hud seemed to hesitate. "I have a witness who saw him fighting with her. It was clear they'd had some type of intimate relationship before that and that Ginger was trying to end it. Jordan broke her wrist. This was soon before her death."

Dana couldn't hide her shock.

"It was apparently an accident. Jordan shoved her, she fell and broke her wrist. The thing is, he lied about his relationship with her and my witness says he paid her to keep quiet about the incident." Hud cursed under his breath as he must have seen something in her expression. "You knew about Ginger and Jordan?"

"Dad told me, but years ago I'd seen Ginger and Jordan in the alley kissing."

Hud swore. "I know Jordan is your brother and even with you being on the outs with him right now, you'd still take up for him when push comes to shove. But, Dana, I'm afraid of what Jordan might be capable of when he doesn't get his way. Right now from what I can gather, what he wants more than anything is the Cardwell Ranch. And you're the only thing standing between him and the money from the sale. Watch your back."

Chapter Ten

Dana had stopped off to see Hilde on the way home, putting off the family meeting as long as possible—and trying to keep her mind off Hud and the kiss and everything he'd told her, as well as the person she'd spotted across the street watching the shop. Watching her.

"Someone is trying to scare me," she told Hilde. "Or worse." She filled her in.

"I'm with Hud. You shouldn't be alone out there. Maybe especially with your family. Come stay with me."

"Thanks, but Hud is coming out later," Dana said. "I really think it's just one of my siblings trying to get me out of the house so they can do a thorough search for Mom's new will."

"Didn't you say you looked for it and couldn't find it?"

Dana nodded. "They would be wasting their time and I could tell them that, but they wouldn't believe me."

"You're sure one of them hasn't already found it?"

"I hope not, because then it is long gone," Dana said. "But then how do I explain these threats?"

"That is too creepy about the doll in the well last night. It sounds like something Jordan would do."

She shook her head. "He wasn't in town." She thought about the doll her father had given her. Why that doll? "I just have a feeling that the person at the well wanted me to see the light and come up and investigate. And I would have, if I hadn't been on the phone with Hud."

"Did he find out who left you the chocolates?"

Dana shook her head. "He's having them checked to see if they might have been poisoned."

Hilde shivered. "Dana, someone came into your house to take that doll and leave the chocolates. That person had to know the house. Not just the house. He knows *you*."

"That's why it's probably one of my siblings." She pulled on her coat. "I kissed Hud."

Hilde's eyebrow shot up. "And?"

"And it was..." She groaned. "Wonderful. Oh, Hilde, I want to believe him. He thinks he was set up five years ago. That someone other than just Stacy wanted to see us broken up and that nothing happened."

"Didn't I tell you that was a possibility?"

Dana nodded.

"You're the only woman he's ever loved," Hilde said. "You know that. Why can't you forgive him?"

"Could you if you caught him in your sister's bed?"

Hilde looked uncertain. "It would be hard. But imagine how he must be feeling? If he really believes nothing happened. Have you ever asked Stacy about it?" Hilde asked.

Dana shook her head. "What was there to ask? You should have seen the expression on her face that morning when I caught them. I can't bear to be in the same room with her, let alone talk to her. And anyway, what was there to ask? 'How was my fiancé?'"

"Given everything that's been going on, maybe this family meeting isn't such a bad idea," Hilde said. "If it was me, I'd corner that sister of yours and demand some answers."

On the way to the ranch, Dana thought about what Hilde had said. How many people knew about the chocolates that Hud had always bought for her birthday? Her family, not that any of them seemed to pay much attention or care. All three of her siblings knew about the doll upstairs and that the ranch house was never locked. But so did a lot of other people.

Stacy, Clay and Jordan seemed the most likely suspects. She couldn't imagine any of them hanging out in a blizzard with a flashlight just to scare her away from the house, though.

But if this wasn't about her siblings trying to speed up the sale of the ranch, then what?

Ginger Adams's murder?

Jordan had always had a terrible temper when he didn't get his way, just as Hud had said.

On top of that, Jordan had lied about his relationship with Ginger Adams—and apparently been so angry when she'd dumped him that he'd knocked her down and broken her wrist. And all this right before she'd ended up in the well.

With a shudder, Dana realized that Jordan also had access to their father's .38. And now the gun was missing.

But that didn't explain the incident last night at the well. Unless Jordan hadn't been in New York when he'd called her yesterday.

As she turned into the ranch house yard, she saw a car parked out front with a rental sticker in the back window. Jordan. Apparently he'd arrived early. She could see lights on in the house and a shadow moving around on the second floor—in what had been their mother's bedroom.

HUD FOUND DEPUTY LIZA STONE waiting for him in his office. "What was so important that you had to see me right away?" he demanded and instantly regretted it. "Sorry."

"Oh, I caught you in the middle of something," she said, stepping tentatively to him to wipe a smudge of lipstick from the corner of his mouth with her thumb. She grinned and he knew he looked sheepish. "But I thought you'd want to see this right away," Liza said, unfazed.

He noticed that her eyes shone with excitement. Then he looked at what she held up. A .38 pistol in a plastic evidence bag. "Where—"

"I was going through the list of names you had me put together, checking to see if I recognized any names on the list of people who owned registered

.38 firearms, when Angus Cardwell drove up." She grinned. "I thought it wouldn't hurt to ask him if he had a .38. He told me he did, but he'd lost it. I asked if he'd mind if I took a look in his truck." Her grin broadened. "Don't worry, I got him to sign a release. And lo and behold, the .38 was right under the seat behind some old rags."

"Nice work, Deputy."

"Tomorrow's my day off," she said quickly. "I was wondering if you'd like me to take the gun up to the crime lab."

"You'd drive all the way to Missoula on your day off?" he asked, amused. She reminded him of the way he'd been when he'd first started working for the sheriff's department.

"Truthfully? I can't stand the suspense," she said. "You should have seen Angus's face when I pulled out the gun— Don't worry, I was careful not to get any of my prints on it. He looked like he might faint. No kidding. He grabbed the side of his pickup. You would have sworn he'd just seen a ghost."

"It might take a while before the lab can run a ballistics test on the pistol," Hud said distractedly, thinking of Angus's reaction.

"I can be pretty persuasive when I need to," Liza said with a grin. "It's about the only advantage of being a woman deputy."

He smiled. Liza was cute, with dark hair, green eyes and freckles. "Call me as soon as you get the results."

"I left the list on your desk," she said as she locked the .38 in the evidence room. "I'll pick it up first thing in the morning."

"One more thing," he said, thinking about what she'd said about being persuasive. "Think you could get the fingerprints of our main suspects before you go off duty?"

She grinned. "Just give me a list."

He jotted down the names: Jordan Cardwell, Clay Cardwell, Angus Cardwell, Stacy Cardwell, Harlan Cardwell. He left off Dana's name. He could get those himself.

She took the list, read down it, then looked at him. "Just about all of the Cardwells, huh?"

He nodded, wishing now that he'd put Dana's name on it.

Liza started for the door. "Oh, I almost forgot. I found a card in that plastic garbage bag with the box of chocolates when I sent it and the doll to the lab for you this morning. I left the card on your desk. And I just took a phone message for you from the airlines regarding the passenger you'd inquired about." Hud could see curiosity burning in her gaze. "Also on your desk."

"Thanks." Hud stepped into his office and picked up the note Liza had left. His heart began to race.

Jordan Cardwell flew in yesterday—not today. He had taken a morning flight. When Dana said he'd called her to let her know he was flying out—he was probably already in the canyon. Maybe even on the ranch.

He picked up the other item Liza had left him. A wadded-up birthday card. He stared at the front. This had been in Dana's wastebasket? He opened the card and saw Stacy's name. His heart stopped dead in his chest.

He recognized this handwriting. Hurriedly, he pulled out the anonymous note he'd received in California. The handwriting matched.

It had been Stacy who'd gotten him back here?

JORDAN MUST HAVE HEARD Dana's pickup approaching because as she parked, the lights upstairs went off. A moment later she saw her brother rush past one of the living room windows.

When she entered the house, he was sitting in one of the overstuffed chairs, one shiny new cowboy boot resting on his opposite leg, a drink in his hand.

"Finally," he said. "I thought you got off at six?"

"Not that it's any of your business, but I had a stop to make. Anyway, Stacy told me the family meeting was at seven," she said, taking off her coat. "Aren't you a little early?"

"I wanted us to visit before the others got here."

She turned to look at him. He was trying to give her the impression he'd been sitting there waiting patiently for her—not upstairs snooping around. Her brother really was a liar. She'd always known that Jordan was a lot of things, but she was starting to worry that he could be a lot more than just a liar. He could be a murderer.

"Visit?" she said, unable to keep the sarcasm out of her voice. "Let me guess what you want to visit about."

"Isn't it possible I might just want to see you before the others arrive?" he demanded. Another lie.

"No. Not unless you want to tell me the truth about what you were doing up in Mother's old room."

He made an ugly face in answer to being found out.

"Or I can tell you," she said against the advice of the little voice in her head warning her to be careful. "You were looking for Mom's will. The one you said didn't exist. In fact, you accused me of making up the story to hold up the sale of the ranch."

"I still believe that."

She felt her anger rise. "If I didn't know better I'd swear you staged that scene last night at the well."

Jordan stared at her. "What are you talking about?"

"Last night," Dana said, biting off each word. "Someone tried to trick me into coming up to the well. To kill me. Or just get me away from the house so you could search for the will. Hud was almost killed."

"I have no idea what you're talking about," Jordan snapped. "Remember? I didn't even fly in until today."

"How do I know you aren't lying again."

Jordan downed the rest of his drink and slammed the glass down on the end table as he launched himself to his feet. "I'm sick of this." He stormed across the room until he stood towering over her. "The ranch is going on the market," he snapped, grabbing both of her shoulders in his hands. "You are going to quit using every legal maneuver possible to hold up the sale."

She tried to pull free, his fingers biting into her flesh.

He gave her a shake. "There is no will. Or if there is, you can't produce it." His words were like the hiss of a snake, his face within inches of hers. "You have no choice, Dana, so stop fighting me or you'll be sorry you were ever born, you stubborn damned—"

The sound of the front door opening killed the rest of his words. He let go of Dana at once and stepped back as Stacy asked, "What's going on?"

"Nothing," Jordan said sullenly. "We were just waiting for you and Clay. Where the hell is Clay, anyway? And what is that?"

Dana never thought she'd be relieved to see her sister. She was also surprised by Stacy's attitude. Her sister never stood up to Jordan but clearly she was angry with him now. Because of what she'd just witnessed?

Her hands trembling, Dana reached for the container in Stacy's hand and instantly regretted taking it.

Through the clear plastic lid she could see the crudely printed words: *Happy Birthday, Dana!* on what was obviously a homemade cake. Stacy had baked?

Dana didn't want to feel touched by the gesture, but she did as she heard the sound of another car coming in from the highway. She realized she and Jordan would have heard Stacy arrive if they hadn't been hollering at each other. Her shoulders still hurt from where he'd grabbed her.

"That must be Clay now," Stacy said, still glaring at Jordan.

He shoved past Stacy and out the front door.

Stacy shrugged out of her coat as she looked around the living room as if she hadn't seen it in a very long time. She hadn't and Dana wondered if her sister might be starting to have doubts about selling the place.

"I wish you hadn't done this," Dana said to her sister, holding up the cake.

"It was nothing," Stacy said, dropping her head.

Dana studied her for a moment wondering if the cake wasn't just a ploy to get back into her good graces so Dana would quit fighting the sale of the ranch. Now that Dana thought about, she wouldn't have been surprised if the cake was Jordan's idea.

Jordan came back in the house, stomping his feet loudly, Clay at his heels.

"Hi, sis," Clay said quietly. He looked as if he might hug her, but changed his mind. He didn't seem to know what to do with his big hands. They fluttered in the air for a moment before he stuffed them into the pockets of his pants. "Happy birthday."

Had he been in on this? He sounded as if he'd only remembered her birthday when he'd seen the cake in her hands, though.

"Hello, Clay." Clay was what was called lanky. He was tall and thin, his bones seeming too large for his body. His hair was shorter than Dana had ever seen it, a buzz cut, and he wore chinos and a T-shirt. He wasn't so much handsome as he was beautiful.

She saw Jordan give him a disgusted look. He'd always thought Clay weak.

Stacy had taken down plates from their mother's good china. Dana watched her stop for a moment as if admiring the pattern. Or maybe she was just speculating on how much the china might be worth on the market.

Their mother should have been here, Dana thought as she watched everyone take a seat around the large table. Jordan pulled out a chair and sat at the spot their mother used to sit. Obviously he now considered himself the head of the family.

Clay sat where he always had, near the other end of the table. Stacy put plates and forks on the table, then took the cake Dana realized she was still holding.

As Dana slumped into her chair, Stacy carefully cut the cake. Dana noticed that her sister's hands were trembling. She served everyone a piece, then started to ask, "Should we sing—"

"No," Dana interrupted. "The cake is more than enough."

Stacy looked disheartened but sat and picked up her fork. "I hope it tastes all right. I don't do much baking."

Jordan snorted at the understatement.

Dana studied her older brother as she took a bite of the cake. What would Jordan have done if Stacy hadn't arrived when she had?

"It's good," Dana said, touched by her sister's kind gesture even though she didn't want to be.

Jordan downed his and shoved his plate and fork aside. "Could we please get this settled now?"

Stacy looked angrily at their brother. "You are such a jerk," she snapped, and got up to take everyone's dishes to the sink.

"Leave the dishes. I'll do them," Dana said, getting up from the table. The kitchen felt too small for this discussion, the smell of chocolate cake too strong. "Let's go in the living room."

They all filed into the adjacent room. Clay sat in the corner, Stacy teetered on the edge of the fireplace hearth, Jordan went straight to the bar and poured himself a drink.

"Dana, you're killing us," Jordan said after gulping down half a glass of her bourbon. "All these attorney fees to fight you. You know we're going to win eventually. So why put us through this?"

Dana looked around the room at each of her siblings. "I can't believe any of you are related to me or Mother. If she knew what you were doing—"

"Don't bring her into this," Jordan snapped. "If she wanted you alone to have the ranch then she should have made the proper arrangements."

"She tried to and you know it," Dana said, fighting not to lose her temper. "I know Mother talked to each of you before she drafted her new will and explained how you would be paid over the long term."

"Produce the document," Jordan demanded.

"You know I can't."

He made an angry swipe through the air. "Then stop fighting us. You can't win and you know it. Dragging your feet has only made things worse. Now we have a dead body on the ranch."

"The body's been there for seventeen years," Dana said. "It would have turned up sooner or later."

"Not if Warren had filled in the well like he was supposed to," Jordan snapped.

Dana narrowed her gaze at him. "You told him to fill in the well?"

Jordan glared at her. "I told him to get the ranch ready to sell. Filling in the well was his idea. How did I know he was going to find human bones in it?"

How indeed?

"We just need to stop fighting among ourselves," Clay said from the corner.

Jordan rolled his eyes. "No, what we need is to get this ranch on the market and hope to hell this investigation is over as quickly as possible. In the meantime, Dana, you could stop being so antagonistic toward the marshal."

Dana felt all the air rush from her lungs as if he'd hit her. "You aren't seriously suggesting that I—"

"Your attitude is making us all look guilty," Jordan said.

"And you think if I'm nice to Hud, it will make you look any less guilty?" she snapped.

"Please, can't we all just quit arguing?" Stacy said, sounding close to tears.

"After the ranch sells, I'm leaving," Clay said out of the blue, making everyone turn to look at him. He seemed embarrassed by the attention. "I have a chance to buy a small theater in Los Angeles."

"You'd leave Montana?" Dana asked, and realized she didn't know her younger brother at all.

Clay gave her a lopsided smile. "You're the one who loves Montana, Dana. I would have left years ago if I could have. And now, with everyone in town talking about our family as if we're murderers... Did you know that a deputy made me stop on the way here to have my fingerprints taken?"

"Stop whining, Clay, I got a call from the deputy, too," Jordan said, and looked at Stacy. She nodded that she had, too.

"What do you expect?" Dana said, tired of her siblings acting so put-upon. "A woman's body was found in our well. We all knew her. She broke up Mom and Dad's marriage. And, Jordan—"

"Maybe Mom killed her and threw her down the well," Jordan interrupted.

The room went deathly quiet.

"Don't give me that look, Dana," he said. "You know Mom was capable of about anything she set her mind to."

"I've heard enough of this," Dana said, and headed for the kitchen.

"Well, that's a surprise," Jordan said to her retreating back. "We knew we couldn't count on you to be reasonable."

Seething with anger, she turned to face him. "I have another month here before the court rules on whether the ranch has to be sold to humor the three of you and I'm taking it. If you don't like it, too bad. I'm fighting to save the ranch my mother loved. All the three of you want is money—any way you can get it. Even by destroying something that has been in our family for generations."

Jordan started to argue but she cut him off. "And as for the murder investigation, you're all on your own. Frankly, I think you're all capable of murder."

Clay and Stacy both denied that they had anything to hide. Jordan just glared at her and said, "You're making a very big mistake, Dana. I hope you don't live to regret it."

She turned and stalked off into the kitchen. Going to the sink, she grabbed the cool porcelain edge and gripped it, Jordan's threat ringing in her ears.

HUD GOT THE CALL FROM the crime lab just as he was starting to leave his office.

"We've found some latent prints on both the box of chocolates and the doll," Dr. Cross said. "I decided to do the tests myself since it tied in with your ongoing case. Interesting case."

"Did you come up with a match?" Hud asked.

"No prints on file that matched any of the prints on the doll or the package. We found multiple prints on the doll, all different. As for the gift, only one set."

Hud felt his heart rate quicken. "My deputy is bringing you up some fingerprints to compare those to. What about the chocolates themselves?"

"No prints on them. Also no sign of a drug or poison. As far as I can tell, they were nothing but chocolate."

Relieved, Hud sighed. "Thanks for doing this so quickly." He hung up. There was one set of prints he hadn't asked Liza to get for him. Lanny Rankin's.

Hud planned to get those himself tonight.

He picked up the phone and started calling the local bars on a hunch. The bartender at the second one Hud called said that Lanny was there.

"Try to keep him there. I'm buying," Hud said. "I'll be right down."

DANA WASN'T SURPRISED to hear tentative footfalls behind her and smell her sister's expensive perfume. Standing at the sink with her back to her sister, she closed her eyes, waiting for the next onslaught. Obviously, Jordan and Clay had sent Stacy in to convince her to change her mind.

"Dana," her sister said quietly. "I have to tell you something."

Dana kept her back turned to her sister. She'd planned on asking her sister point-blank what had happened that night five years ago with Hud. But quite frankly, she just wasn't up to the answer tonight.

"You can't just keep ignoring me. I'm your sister."

"Don't remind me," Dana said, finally giving up and turning to look at her.

Tears welled in Stacy's eyes, but she bit her lip to stem them, no doubt realizing that tears would only anger Dana more. Likewise another apology.

"I have to tell you the truth," Stacy said.

"Don't," Dana said. "I told you, I don't want to hear anything you have to say. I know they sent you in here to try to get me to change my mind."

"I didn't come in here to talk about the ranch," she said, and sounded surprised that Dana would think that. "I need to tell you about Hud."

Dana felt her face flush. "I'd rather talk about selling the ranch." She started to step past Stacy, but her sister touched her arm and whispered, "I lied."

Dana froze, her gaze leaping to Stacy's face.

Her sister nodded slowly, the tears in her eyes spilling over. "I didn't sleep with him," she whispered, and looked behind her as if afraid their brothers might be listening.

"What is this? Some ploy to get me to sell the ranch?" Dana couldn't believe how low her sister would stoop.

"This doesn't have anything to do with the ranch." Stacy shook her head, tears now spilling down her cheeks. "I have to tell you the truth, no matter what happens to me. I didn't want to do it."

Dana felt her pulse jump. "What are you talking about?" she asked, remembering what Hud had said about Stacy not acting alone that night.

Stacy gripped her arm. "I didn't have a choice."

"You always have a choice," Dana said, keeping her voice down. "What happened that night?"

Stacy looked scared as she let go of Dana and glanced over her shoulder again.

"Don't move," Dana ordered, and walked to the doorway to the living room. "Leave," she said to Jordan and Clay. Clay got up at once but Jordan didn't move.

"We're not finished here," Jordan said angrily. "And I'm not leaving until this is settled. One way or the other."

"Stacy and I need to talk," Dana said, letting him believe she had to iron things out with her sister before she would give in on selling the ranch.

Clay was already heading for the door as Jordan reluctantly rose. Clay opened the front door then stopped. Dana saw why. Their father's pickup had just pulled into the yard.

"I'll be outside talking to Dad," Jordan said, and practically shoved Clay out the door.

What was their father doing here? Dana wondered as she hurried back to the kitchen. No doubt her siblings had commandeered his help to convince her to sell the ranch. Bastards.

Stacy had sat at the table, her head in her hands. Dana closed the kitchen door as she heard her brothers and their father talking out on the porch. It almost sounded as if Jordan and Angus were arguing.

What was that about? She'd find out soon enough, she feared. But right now she wanted some answers out of her sister.

Stacy looked up when Dana closed the kitchen door. "I'm so sorry."

"Don't start that again. Just tell me." Dana didn't sit. She stood, her arms folded across her chest to keep her hands from shaking, to keep from strangling Stacy. "Tell me *everything* and whatever you do, don't lie to me."

Stacy started to cry. "I'm telling you I didn't sleep with Hud, isn't that enough?"

"No. I need to know how he got there. Did he pick you up at the bar? Or did you pick him up?"

Stacy was crying harder. "I picked him up."

"How?" Hud swore he'd had only one drink. But she recalled hearing from people at the bar that night that he'd been falling-down drunk when he'd left with Stacy.

"I drugged him."

Dana stared at her sister in disbelief. "You drugged him!"

"I had to do it!" she cried. "Then before the drug could completely knock him out, I got him outside and into my car."

Dana could hear raised voices now coming from the living room. The three had brought their argument in out of the cold. But the fact barely registered. Stacy had admitted that she'd drugged Hud and taken him out to her car.

"I was to take him to my place," Stacy said, the words tumbling out with the tears. "I thought that was all I had to do. I didn't want to do it. I swear. But if I didn't..." She began to sob. Angus and Jordan were yelling at each other in the living room, the words incomprehensible.

"What did you do?" Dana demanded, moving to stand over her.

"I didn't know part of the plan was to make it look like we'd slept together until when you got there the next morning," Stacy cried. "I didn't want to hurt you."

Dana remembered the look of shock on Hud's and Stacy's faces when they'd seen her that morning. She'd thought it was from being caught. But now she recalled it was bewilderment, as well.

"Why tell me now?" Dana demanded. "Why not tell me five years ago before you ruined everything?"

"I couldn't. I was scared. I'm still scared, but I can't live like this anymore." Stacy looked up, her gaze meeting her sister's. The fear was as real as the anguish, Dana thought. "I've hated myself for what I did. No matter what happens to me now, I had to tell you. I couldn't live with what I did."

"What do you mean, no matter what happens to you now?"

Stacy shook her head. "I used to be afraid of going to jail, but even that is better than the hell I've been in these past years. I'm not strong like you. I couldn't stand up to them."

Them? "Jail?" Dana repeated. For just an instant she flashed again on the memory of Stacy's face that morning five years ago. Stacy had looked scared. Or was it trapped? "Are you telling me someone was threatening jail if you didn't go along with setting Hud up?"

The kitchen door banged open and Clay appeared, panicked and breathless. "It's Dad. I think he's having a heart attack!"

Chapter Eleven

Lanny Rankin was anything but happy to see Hud take the stool next to him at the bar.

The lawyer had two drinks in front of him and was clearly on his way to getting drunk.

"What do you want?" Lanny slurred.

"Just thought I'd have a drink." Hud signaled the bartender who brought him a draft beer from the tap. He took a drink and watched Lanny pick up his glass and down half of what appeared to be a vodka tonic.

"Bring Lanny another drink," Hud told the bartender.

Lanny shoved his glass away and picked up the second drink and downed it, as well, before stumbling to his feet. "Save your money, Marshal. I'm not drinking with you."

"I hope you're not driving," Hud said.

Lanny narrowed his gaze. "You'd love to arrest me, wouldn't you? She tell you about us? Is that what you're doing here? Tell you we're engaged? Well, it's all a lie. All a lie." His face turned mean. "She's all yours. But then again, she always has been, hasn't she?"

He turned and stumbled out the back door.

Hud quickly pulled an evidence bag from his jacket pocket and slipped both of the glasses with Lanny's prints on them inside. He paid his bill and went outside to make sure Lanny wasn't driving anywhere.

Lanny was walking down the street toward his condo.

Hud watched him for a moment, then headed for his office. If he hurried, he could get both glasses ready for Liza to take to the crime lab in the morning.

He wondered if Liza had any trouble getting the Cardwell clan's fingerprints.

Just the thought of the family meeting going on at the ranch made him uneasy. Maybe he would swing by there after he'd sent the glasses to the lab.

Back at his office, Hud got the drink glasses with Lanny's prints ready and locked the box in the evidence room with the .38 Liza had taken from Angus's pickup.

As he started to leave, he remembered the list of registered owners of .38 pistols in the county Liza had left on his desk. The list was long. He thumbed through it, his mind more on the family meeting going on at the Cardwell Ranch than the blur of names.

This list had probably been a waste of time. There was a very good chance that Liza had already found the murder weapon and it was now locked in the evidence room. By tomorrow, Hud worried that he would be arresting Angus Cardwell. He didn't even want to think what that would do to Dana.

He folded the list and stuck it in his pocket. As he started to leave, planning to go out and check on Dana, no matter how angry it made her, he heard the call come in on the scanner. An ambulance was needed at the Cardwell Ranch.

"How's Dad?" Dana asked when she found Jordan and Clay in the waiting room at Bozeman Deaconess Hospital. She hadn't been able to get any information at the desk on her way in and the roads down the canyon had been icy, traffic slow.

Clay shrugged, looking miserable and nervous in a corner chair.

"The doctor's in with him," Jordan said, pacing the small room, clearly agitated.

"Where's Stacy?" she asked. Earlier Dana had glanced through the open living room doorway and seen her father on the floor, Jordan leaning over him. She'd let out a cry and run into the living room. Behind her she'd heard Clay on the phone calling for an ambulance on the kitchen phone.

It wasn't until later, after the ambulance had rushed Angus to the hospital and Dana began looking for her keys to follow in her pickup, that she'd realized Stacy was gone.

"When did Stacy leave?" Dana asked, glancing around.

Both brothers shrugged. "After I called 9-1-1 I turned around and I noticed your back door was open, and when I went out to follow the ambulance, I saw that her car was already gone."

"Stacy just left?" Dana asked in disbelief. Why would her sister do that without a word? Especially with their father in the next room on the floor unconscious?

Stacy's words echoed in Dana's ears. "No matter what happens to me now." Was it possible her sister was in danger because she'd told Dana the truth?

Dana couldn't worry about that now. "What were you and Dad fighting about?" she asked Jordan.

"This is not my fault," Jordan snapped.

"I'll get us some coffee," Clay said, and practically bolted from the room.

Jordan and Angus couldn't have been arguing about the sale of the ranch. Her father had said he wasn't going to take sides, but he did add that he felt the ranch was too much for Dana to handle on her own.

"Sell it, baby girl," he'd said to Dana. "It's an albatross around your neck. Your mother would understand."

"That's how you felt about the ranch, Dad, not me," she'd told him.

But he'd only shook his head and said, "Sell it. Some day you'll be glad you did. And it will keep peace in the family." He'd always been big on keeping peace in the family. Except when it came to his wandering ways.

"I heard the two of you yelling at each other in the other room," Dana said. "What was going on?"

Jordan stopped pacing to look at her. "The stupid fool thinks I killed Ginger."

Ginger Adams, the woman whose wrist he'd broken in an argument. The woman who'd ended up in the Cardwell Ranch well. The floor under her seemed to give way. "Why would Dad think that?"

"Who the hell knows? He's always been a crazy old fool."

Dana bristled. "Dad is a lot of things. Crazy isn't one of them."

Jordan's look was lethal. "Don't play games with me. Dad told me you knew about me and Ginger. What's crazy is that he thinks I took his gun."

She stared at him. "The missing .38?"

"Turns out it wasn't missing," Jordan said. "It was under the seat of his pickup and now the cops have it. He thinks I took the gun and then when Ginger's body was found, I put it under the pickup seat to frame him for her murder."

Dana felt her heart drop to her feet. Hadn't Hud told her that the gun was used in both Ginger's murder and Judge Randolph's? What motive could Jordan have to kill the judge, though? "Jordan, you didn't—"

Jordan let out a curse. "You think I'm a murderer, too?" His angry gaze bore into her. "Not only a murderer, but I framed my own father, as well?" He let out a scornful laugh and shook his head at her. "I guess I didn't realize how little you and Dad thought of me until now." He turned and stormed out of the waiting room, almost colliding with Clay who was carrying a cardboard tray with three cups of coffee on it.

What bothered Dana was the guilty look in Jordan's eyes before he left.

"Thanks," she said as she took one of the foam cups of hot coffee Clay offered her and stepped out in the hallway, fighting the terrible fear that had settled in the pit of her stomach.

At the sound of footfalls, she turned to see her father's doctor coming toward her. She froze. All she could think about was the day of her mother's accident and the doctor coming down the hall to give her the news. She couldn't lose another parent.

HUD SPOTTED DANA THE MOMENT he walked into the Bozeman hospital emergency room waiting area. Relief washed through him, making his legs feel boneless. She was all right.

She was talking to the doctor and he could see the concern in her face. He waited, studying her body language, fear closing his throat.

Her shoulders seemed to slump, and he saw her hand go to her mouth then brush at her tears. She was smiling and nodding, and Hud knew that whatever had happened, there had been good news.

She saw him then. He tried not to read anything into her expression. For a moment there she'd actually looked glad to see him.

She said something to the doctor and walked toward him. He caught his breath. Sometimes he forgot how beautiful she was. Her eyes were bright, cheeks flushed from crying, her face glowing with the good news the doctor had given her.

"Dana?" he said as she closed the distance. "What's happened?"

"Dad. He had a heart attack." Her voice broke. "But the doctor says he's stable now." She looked up at him, tears in her eyes. "I have to talk to you."

"Okay." He couldn't help but sound tentative. She hadn't wanted to lay eyes on him—let alone talk to him. "Did you want to talk at the office or—"

She glanced around, making him wonder where her brothers were. And Stacy. "Could we go back to your place?"

His place? "Sure." Whatever she wanted to talk to him about was serious. "You want to follow me?"

She shook her head. "I need to stop by Stacy's. You go on. I'll meet you there."

Whatever that was about he didn't want to know. But at the same time, he didn't like the idea of her going alone.

"I could go with you," he said.

She shook her head again. "I'll meet you at the cabin you're renting." She knew where he lived?

"I'll see you soon," he said.

She nodded distractedly. "Soon."

As he got into his patrol car, he tried not to even guess what this was about. But he had a bad feeling it could have something to do with her father's gun now locked in his evidence cabinet at the office.

The night was clear, stars bright dots in the crystalline cold blue of the sky overhead. Snow covered everything. It sat in puffy white clumps in the branches of the trees and gleamed in the starlight like zillions of diamonds on the open field across the road.

The drive home was interminable. He kept looking in his rearview mirror, hoping to see the headlights of Dana's pickup. She'd said she needed to make a stop by Stacy's. He wished he'd asked how long she might be.

He parked in front of the cabin, the night darker than the inside of a gunny sack. In the cabin, he straightened up, built a fire and put on some coffee.

A wind had come up. It whirled the light fresh snow in a blizzard of white outside the window. He should have insisted she ride with him as upset as she was. But he'd had no desire to go to Stacy's, and Dana hadn't wanted him along.

The sky over the tops of the pines darkened as another storm moved in. He'd forgotten how dark it could be in the dead of winter.

He watched the road—what little of it he could see through the swirling snow. Surprisingly he really had missed winters while in Los Angeles. Missed the seasons that were so dramatic in Montana. Especially winter. Two feet of snow could fall overnight. It wasn't unusual to wake up to the silence and the cold and know that something had changed during the night.

Dana should be here by now. He began to worry, thinking about what he'd heard in her voice. She'd been upset about her father. But that hadn't been all of it. Something had happened. Something she needed to talk to him about. But first she had to see Stacy.

Hud was to the point where he was ready to go looking for her when he spotted headlights through the drifting snow.

She pulled in beside his patrol car and got out, seeming to hesitate. She was wearing a red fleece jacket, her dark hair tucked up under a navy stocking cap. A few strands whipped around her face as she stared at the cabin.

He opened the front door and stood looking at her. A small drift had formed just outside the door and now ran across the porch. The steps down had disappeared, the snow smooth and deep.

He met her gaze through dancing snowflakes, then reached for the shovel. But before he could clean off the steps, she was coming up them, all hesitation gone.

To his utter shock, she rushed to him. He took her in his arms, now truly afraid.

"I'm sorry." Her words were barely audible over the howl of the wind across the roof. "I'm so sorry."

He held her, his heart in his throat. He hugged her to him, breathing in the smell of her. God, how he'd missed that scent. But what could she possibly be sorry about?

Holding her felt so good, he hated it when she stepped from his arms and went inside the cabin. He followed, closing the door to the wind and snow.

She had walked to the fireplace. When she turned, he saw the tears. Dana crying. He could count on one hand the times he'd seen that. His fear escalated.

"Whatever it is, I'll help you," he said, wanting to hold her again but afraid to step toward her.

She let out a laugh at his words and shook her head. Her face was flushed, her eyes bright. "I haven't killed anyone. Although it did cross my mind." She sobered, her gaze locked on his. "I talked to my sister."

His heart dislodged from his throat and dropped to his stomach.

She jerked her cap from her head, shaking off the snow as her hair fell around her shoulders. "She told me everything."

He didn't move—didn't breathe. He'd told himself that he'd come back here to learn everything that had happened that night but now he wasn't so sure he wanted to know.

"You were right. She lied. She was sent to the bar to drug you, get you out of there before the drug completely knocked you out and take you to her place. It was just as you suspected—" her voice broke, eyes shimmering with tears "—nothing happened. You *were* set up." A tear trailed down her cheek. "*We* were set up."

It took him a moment. So it had been just as he'd believed in his heart. No matter how drunk he might have been, he wouldn't have bedded Dana's sister or any other woman for that matter. He'd known it. And yet he'd feared that for that night, he'd lost his mind and his way.

"I'm so sorry I didn't believe you. That I didn't even give you a chance to explain."

He found himself shaking with relief and anger as he stepped to Dana and pulled her into his arms again. "I couldn't have explained it. That's why I left. I thought it would be easier on you if you never had to see me again."

"But you came back."

"Thanks to your sister."

Dana raised her head to look into his face. "Stacy sent you the note?"

He nodded. "I found the birthday card she mailed you, the one you'd thrown away. It was under the box of chocolates. I recognized the handwriting."

"So she was responsible for you coming back." She leaned into him again.

He rested his chin on the top of her head. Her hair felt like silk. Her body softened against his. He could feel his heart pounding. Nothing had happened that night. He closed his eyes and pulled Dana even closer, wishing he could turn back the clock. These wasted years apart felt like a chasm between them.

"I SHOULD HAVE TRUSTED YOU." Dana hadn't believed that he'd been set up, that nothing had happened. She hadn't loved him enough. If she'd trusted him, if she'd even let him tell her his side of the story...

"Hey, there were times I didn't believe in my innocence myself," he said, holding her at arm's length to look into her face. "I thought maybe I'd lost my mind. Or worse, that I was about to become my father."

The blaze in the fireplace popped and cracked, the flames throwing shadows on the walls. She could hear the wind howling outside. Snow hit the windows, sticking, then melting down. Inside, the fire burned. Outside, the storm raged, the snow piling deeper and deeper.

She looked up into Hud's eyes and saw nothing but love. All her anger at herself and her sister melted like the snow at the windows.

She covered one of his hands with her own, turning the palm up to kiss the warm center. She heard him let out a breath. Their eyes locked, the heat of his look warming her to her core.

"Oh, Hud," she breathed. She heard his breath catch, saw the spark of desire catch fire in his eyes. "I've never stopped wanting you."

He groaned and took her with a kiss, his mouth capturing hers as he tugged her even closer to him. She could feel the pounding of his heart, felt her body melt into his.

"I didn't want to live without you," he said as he pulled back. "The only way I was able to get through the past five years was to believe that you still loved me."

She touched his cheek, then cupped his face in her hands and kissed him, teasing the tip of his tongue with her own.

He moaned against her lips, then swept her up into his arms, carrying her to the rug in front of the fire.

She pulled him down to her. His kiss was gentle and slow, as if they had all night to make love. They did.

"You are so beautiful," he whispered, his hand trailing down the length of her neck. He leaned in to kiss her, his hand cupping her breast, and she groaned with the exquisite pleasure of his touch.

The fire warmed her skin as he slowly unbuttoned her blouse and pressed his lips to the hard nipple of one breast, then the other. She arched against him, her fingers working at the buttons of his shirt.

Their clothes began to pile up in the corner as the fire popped and crackled, the heat shimmering over their naked bodies, damp with perspiration and wet warm kisses.

Their lovemaking was all heat and fire, a frenzied rush of passion that left them both breathless.

Hud held her, smoothing her hair under his hand, his eyes locked with hers as their bodies cooled.

Dana looked into his eyes, still stunned by the powerful chemistry that arced between them. Nothing had killed it. Not the pain, not the years.

She curled into his strong arms and slept. On this night, no wind woke her with a premonition. She had no warning what the day would bring. If only for one night, she felt safe. She felt loved.

Chapter Twelve

Dana drove to Bozeman to the hospital before daylight the next morning. Her father was still in stable condition, sedated and sleeping. She peeked in on him and then drove back to Big Sky and the shop.

She spent the quiet early morning before the shop opened unloading the latest shipment of fabric and pricing it. Unfortunately the task wasn't difficult enough that it kept her from thinking about last night with Hud.

She wasn't surprised when she heard a knock at the back door and saw him.

"Good morning," he said, but his look said there was nothing good about it.

"Good morning." She couldn't believe how glad she was to see him. She'd never stopped being in love with him and even when she hadn't known the truth, he'd been much harder to hate in the flesh than he'd been in her memory.

He pulled off his hat to rake his fingers through his thick sandy-blond hair. It was a nervous habit. She felt a jolt, wondering what he had to be nervous about.

"You left before I woke up this morning," he said.

She nodded sheepishly. "I needed to think about some things and go see my father."

"Think about some things?"

She sighed, picking up a bolt of fabric and carrying it over to its spot on the wall. "About last night."

"You're afraid I'm going to hurt you again?" he asked behind her.

She turned and looked up into his wonderful face. "Do you blame me? You left me for five years."

"But if you believe that Stacy was finally telling the truth—"

"I do, but…"

"You still can't forget," he said softly.

She reached up to cup his rough jaw. He hadn't taken the time to shave. Instead he'd rushed right over here. "Last night made me feel all those old wonderful feelings again that we shared."

"You know I came back here because of you. Because I still love you. I'm sorry I didn't come back sooner. I should never have left."

"You thought you'd lost everything, your career—"

"Losing you is what devastated my life, Dana. It took a while to get my head on straight."

She nodded. "I just need to take it slow." She dropped her hand and turned her back to him. Otherwise, she would be in his arms and Hilde would find them between racks of fabric making love on the hardwood floor when she came in.

"We can take it as slow as you need," he said. "Just don't push me away again." He pulled her around to face him and into his arms, kissing her until she was breathless.

She leaned into his strong, hard body and rested her cheek against his chest, his jacket open, his cotton shirt warm and soft. She could hear his heart beating fast and realized she'd scared him with her disappearing act this morning.

"I'm sorry I took off this morning," she said against his chest.

He hugged her tighter. "I know you're worried about your dad. And Stacy." He sighed. "Dana, I found out that your brother Jordan got into town the day of your birthday."

She pulled back a little to look at him. "He lied about that, too?"

Hud nodded. "I'm sorry, but I think he's responsible for what happened at the well the night before last, and if he is, I'm going to have to arrest him."

She made a sound deep down in her throat as she realized that most of her family could end up in jail the way things were going. "Hud, you and I both know that if Jordan had found those bones in the well he'd have covered them with fifteen feet of dirt and never given them another thought."

Blood was thicker than water. But this was Hud and the truth was the truth.

"And don't try to make me sound so noble," she said. "I didn't tell you everything." She told him about going to see her father about his .38, then about finding Jordan searching the ranch house and finally that

Jordan and her father had been arguing just before Angus Cardwell's collapse. "Is Dad's .38 the murder weapon?" she asked, her heart in her throat.

"We don't know yet. But I'm worried. I'd like you to drive out with me to talk to Stacy."

"When I stopped by her place last night on the way to your cabin," Dana said, "she wasn't there."

"Maybe she's come back. Or maybe she left something behind that will give us an idea of where she's gone. If what she told you is true, then someone was behind setting me up. I need to know who it was. And why. If she was being threatened with jail, then, Dana, I have a pretty good idea who was behind it. I just have to prove it. I need your help. Your sister might open up if we're there together."

As if on cue, Hilde came in the back door on a gust of wind. She looked surprised to see Dana at work so early and even more surprised to see Hud. She looked from one to the other, her gaze finally settling on Dana. She smiled, obviously seeing what Dana had hoped to keep a secret.

"Hello, Hud," Hilde said.

"Nice to see you again, Hilde," he said. "I just came by to steal your partner for a little while."

"Be my guest," Hilde said, giving Dana a meaningful look.

"We're just going to look for Stacy," Dana said. "It's a long story."

"I'm sure it is," Hilde said, still smiling.

Dana groaned inwardly. Her friend knew her too well. Hilde had seen the glow in her cheeks this morning, the sparkle in her eye. Hud had always been able to put it there. "Let me get my coat."

SNOW WAS PILED HIGH on each side of the highway. Beside it, the river gurgled blue-green under a thick skin of transparent ice.

"You're sure she said 'jail'?"

Dana nodded. "She looked scared, Hud. I guess that's why I believed her. She seemed to think she was in danger."

"I think she set me up to keep me away from Judge Randolph's house that night," Hud said. "It's the only thing that makes any sense."

"You think Stacy had something to do with the judge's murder?"

"Look at the evidence, Dana. The judge was murdered the same night Stacy drugged me at the bar and made sure I wasn't the one who responded to the call about shots fired at the Randolph house. Instead, my father took the call. Or at least that's the story."

"What are you saying, Hud? You can't seriously think your own father was behind it."

"Stacy was being threatened with jail, isn't that what she said? Now she seems to be running scared." Hud glanced over at Dana. "I think she's afraid because she knows the truth about that night."

"You can't believe your father killed the judge."

He sighed. "I don't know what I believe. The judge had Alzheimer's. He was about to be asked to step down from the bench. Unless he had hard evidence against Brick, then the judge wasn't really a threat."

"So then your father had no motive."

"So it would seem," Hud said as he turned off Jackrabbit Road onto Cameron Bridge Road.

"Maybe the fact that the judge was killed that night was just a coincidence," Dana said.

He wished he could believe that.

Stacy was in between husbands right now and living in the house she was awarded in the divorce settlement from Emery Chambers. The divorce that, according to Lanny, Hud had helped her get.

"It has to be about more than just splitting us up. Who would care enough to go to all that trouble?" Hud said.

"Stacy for one."

"What about Lanny?" He saw Dana shiver. "What?"

"When he heard you were back in town he was very angry."

Hud rubbed his still sore jaw. "I noticed."

He drove a few miles down the river before turning into a graveled yard in front of a large older house. There were no fresh tracks in the snow. No one had been in or out since Dana had stopped by last night.

Through the windows in the garage, Dana could see that Stacy's car was still gone.

"Let's give it a try anyway," Hud said, and opened his door.

Dana followed him up the unshoveled walk and waited while he knocked. Through the trees, he could see an open hole in the ice on the Gallatin River, the water a deep, clear green. The air smelled of fresh snow and cottonwoods.

He knocked again, then turned to see Dana bend to pick up something from the snow beside the front step. A black glove.

"It's one of the cashmere gloves my sister was wearing yesterday when she came to the house."

His mouth went dry. Stacy had come back here after the family meeting, then left again?

He reached for the doorknob. It turned in his hand, the door swinging into the empty living room. He signaled Dana to wait as he moved quickly through the house, weapon drawn. Something about the empty feel of the house made him fear he wasn't going to find Stacy. At least not alive.

Upstairs, the bedroom looked as if a bomb had gone off in it.

"It's clear," he called down to Dana.

"My God," Dana said as she saw the room, the drawers hanging open and empty, clothes hangers on the floor or cocked at an odd angle as if the clothing had been ripped from them.

She moved to the closet and touched one of the dresses that had been left behind. "She's either running scared or someone wants us to believe she is."

He nodded, having already come to the same conclusion. If Stacy was as scared as Dana had said and decided to blow town, she would have grabbed just what she needed. Or left without anything. She wouldn't have tried to take everything. Or would she? Maybe she wasn't planning to ever come back.

"Who are you calling?" Dana asked, sounding worried.

"I'm going to have some deputies search the wooded area behind the house," he said. "Just as a precaution."

Dana nodded, but he saw that she feared the same thing he did. That Stacy had been telling the truth. Her life had been in danger.

While they waited for the deputies to arrive and search the woods around the house, they searched the house again, looking for anything that would give them a clue.

They found nothing.

"Do you want me to take you home?" Hud offered.

Dana shook her head. "Please just take me back to the shop."

"Hilde's working with you all day, right?" Hud asked.

"Yes, I'll be fine. We both have work to do. And maybe Stacy will contact me."

He nodded. "I just don't want you alone. Especially now with your sister missing." His cell phone rang.

It was Roadside Café owner and former cook Leroy Perkins. "You were asking about Ginger's old roommate the other day," Leroy said. "I finally remembered her name. Zoey Skinner. I asked around. You'd be surprised how much cooks know about what's going on. The good ones anyway can cook *and* listen." He laughed. "Zoey's working at a café in West Yellowstone. The Lonesome Pine Café."

"Thanks." Hud broke the connection and looked over at Dana. "I need to go up to West Yellowstone. I'll be back before you get off work." He hesitated. "I was hoping we could have dinner together."

"Is that what you were hoping?" she asked with a smile.

"Actually, I was hoping you would come back to the cabin tonight. I could pick up some steaks... But maybe that's moving too fast for you." He gave her an innocent grin. "I can't stand having you out of my sight."

"I told you I'll be safe at the shop," she said.

"I wasn't thinking of your safety."

She met his gaze and felt that slow burn in her belly. "Dinner at your cabin sounds wonderful. I just need to go home and feed Joe."

"I'll stop off and feed Joe and then pick you up at the shop," he suggested.

She knew he just didn't want her going back to the ranch house. The thought of it did make her uncomfortable, but it was still her home—a home she was fighting to keep. "I at least need to go out to the ranch and pick up some clothes. Why don't you meet me there?"

She could see he didn't like that idea.

"I'll be waiting for you at your house," he said.

She didn't argue. She felt safe believing that no one would attack either her or Hud in broad daylight. But once it got dark, she would think again of the doll in the well and remember that she was more than likely the target. It chilled her to the bone to think of what could have happened if she hadn't gone up there with the shotgun.

"Just be careful, okay?" Hud said.

"You, too." She touched his cheek and ached to be in his arms again. Whose fool idea was it to take things slow?

As HUD PULLED INTO THE LAKE house, he found his father shoveling snow.

"I don't see you for years then I see you twice in two days?" Brick said with a shake of his head as Hud got out of the patrol car.

Brick set aside the snow shovel he'd been using on the walk. "I suppose you want to talk. It's warmer inside."

Without a word, Hud followed.

"I could make some coffee," Brick said, shrugging out of his coat at the door.

"No need." Hud stood just inside, not bothering to take off his boots or his coat. He wouldn't be staying long.

Brick slumped down onto the bench by the door and worked off his boots. He seemed even smaller today in spite of all the winter clothing he wore. He also seemed stoved-up as if just getting his boots off hurt him but that he was trying hard not to let Hud see it.

"So what's on your mind?" Brick said. "If it's about the robbery again—"

"It's about Stacy Cardwell."

Brick looked up from unlacing his boots, cocking his head as if he hadn't heard right. "What about her?"

"She admitted that she helped set me up the night the judge was killed five years ago."

Brick lifted a brow. "And you believe her?" He let his boot drop to the floor with a thud as he rose and walked stocking-footed toward the kitchen.

"She said she did it so she wouldn't have to go to jail," he said, raising his voice as he spoke to his father's retreating back.

Brick didn't turn, didn't even acknowledge that he'd heard. Hud could hear him in the kitchen running water. He stood for a moment, the snow on his boots melting onto the stone entryway. "Did you hear me?"

"I heard you." Brick appeared in the kitchen doorway, an old-fashioned percolator coffeepot in his hand. "I'm going to make coffee. You might as well come on in. You can't hurt the floor." He turned his back, disappearing into the kitchen again.

"Well?" Hud said after he joined him. The kitchen was neater than it had been yesterday. He wondered if his father had cleaned it because of Hud's visit.

"Sit down," Brick said, but Hud remained standing.

"Were you the one behind coercing Stacy to set me up?" Hud demanded.

Brick turned to look at him. "Why would I do that?"

"To keep me from marrying Dana."

"Falling for Dana Cardwell was the only smart thing you ever did. Why wouldn't I want you to marry her?"

"Then you did it to get to the judge. You just wanted me out of the way so you used me, not caring what it would do to my life."

His father frowned and turned back to the stove. The coffee began to perk, filling the small house with a rich, warm aroma that reminded Hud of all the mornings his father had gotten up to make coffee over the years, especially when Hud's mother was sick.

"Why would Stacy make up something like that?" Hud asked.

"Why does Stacy do half the things she does?" Brick turned, still frowning. "She said she did it to keep herself out of jail?" He shook his head. "I never picked her up for anything. Maybe she did something she thought she would be arrested for and someone found out about it."

"You mean, blackmail?" Hud asked. Clearly he hadn't considered that.

Brick nodded. "Hadn't thought of that, huh? Something else you probably haven't considered is who else had the power to make a threat like that stick." Brick smiled and nodded. "That's right. Judge Raymond Randolph."

Hud felt the air rush out of him. "That doesn't make any sense. Why would the judge get her to keep me out of the picture?" A thought struck him. "Unless the judge wanted to make sure you responded to the call."

His father raised a brow. "You think he staged it so I'd show up and then what? He'd kill me?" Brick shook his head. "I wouldn't put it past him. Especially since he was losing his mind. But that would mean it backfired on him if that were the case and, no matter what you think, I didn't kill the judge."

"It seems more likely that I was set up so someone could use it as a way to get to the judge," Hud said.

"I agree. But you're just barking up the wrong tree if you think it was me. No matter how strongly I felt about you not staying in law enforcement, I would never set you up to get rid of you. I'm sorry you believe I would."

"I hope that's true," Hud said, and realized he meant it. He started for the door.

"Sure you don't want some coffee? It's almost ready."

"No thanks."

"Son."

Hud stopped at the door and turned to look back at his father.

Brick stood silhouetted against the frozen lake through this front window. "Be careful. It sounds like you've got at least one killer out there. Someone who thought they'd gotten away with murder. It's easier to kill after the first time, they say." His father turned back to his coffee.

IN BETWEEN CUSTOMERS, Dana told Hilde about everything else that had happened, including Stacy's confession—and disappearance.

"I can't believe this," Hilde said. "I mean, I do believe it. I never thought Hud would ever betray you. He just isn't that kind of man."

"Why didn't I see that?" Dana said, still feeling guilty and ashamed she hadn't given the man she loved a chance to even explain.

"Because you were too close to it," her friend said. "Any woman would have reacted the same way. If I would have found my man in bed with another woman, I would have shot first and asked questions later."

Dana smiled, knowing that Hilde was just trying to make her feel better.

"Oh, darn," Hilde said.

"What is it?"

"Mrs. Randolph. She left her fabric package."

Dana laughed. "She came back to the shop again? Don't tell me. She was still looking for the perfect blue thread to match those slacks of hers."

"No," Hilde said on a sigh. "This time she bought fabric for some aprons she was making for some charity event. She said you were going to help her with it?"

Dana groaned. Had she volunteered to make aprons? "Let me run it over to her. I need to find out what I've gotten myself into this time."

"Are you sure? Didn't Hud say that you weren't to leave here alone?"

Dana shook her head at her friend. "I'm just going up the canyon as far as the Randolph house. I will be back in twenty minutes tops. And, anyway, you have bookkeeping to do. It makes more sense for me to go since you're the one with the head for figures."

Hilde laughed. "You just don't want to do this. Can't fool me." She handed her the package. "Good luck. Who knows what Kitty Randolph will talk you into before you get back."

"She always tells me how close she and my mother were and how much I look like my mother and how my mother would love that I'm working on fundraisers with her now."

"You're just a girl who can't say no," Hilde joked.

"That's probably why I agreed to have dinner at Hud's cabin tonight." She grinned at her friend on her way out.

The highway had been plowed and sanded in the worst areas so the drive to Kitty Randolph's was no problem. It felt good to get out for a while.

Dana hadn't been completely honest, though, with her friend. There was another reason she wanted to see Mrs. Randolph. She wanted to ask her about something she'd heard that morning from one of the customers.

Nancy Harper had come in to buy drapery fabric and had mentioned seeing Stacy last night.

"What time was this?" Dana had asked, trying not to sound too interested and get the gossip mill going.

"Must have been about nine," Nancy said. "She drove past. I saw her brake in front of Kitty Randolph's house." Nancy smiled. "Is your sister helping with the clinic fundraiser? I knew you were, but I was a little surprised Stacy had volunteered. She's never shown much interest in that sort of thing, not after that one she helped with. And this fundraiser is going to involve cooking and sewing."

Dana had joined Nancy in a chuckle while cringing inside at everyone's perception of her sister. "You're right, that doesn't sound much like my sister."

"Well, you know Kitty. She can be very persuasive."

"You're sure it was Stacy?" Dana had asked, convinced Nancy had to be mistaken. Stacy had helped with one fundraiser years ago while she was between husbands. By the end of the event, Stacy wasn't speaking to Kitty. The two had stayed clear of each other ever since from what Dana could tell.

"Oh, it was Stacy, all right," Nancy said. "I didn't see her get out of her car because my view was blocked by the trees. But I saw her behind the wheel and I recognized the way she drives. She really does drive too fast for road conditions." Her smile said it was too bad Stacy wasn't more like Dana.

As Dana drove past Nancy Harper's house and parked in front of the Randolph house, the only other house on the dead-end road, she wondered again why Stacy would have come here last night. If indeed she did.

The double garage doors to Kitty's house were closed and there were no visible windows so she could see if Kitty was home or not. Getting out, she walked up the freshly shoveled steps and rang the doorbell.

No answer. She rang the bell again and thought she heard a thud from inside the house. Her first thought was that the elderly woman had been hurrying to the door and fallen.

"Mrs. Randolph?" she called, and knocked on the door. She tried the knob. The door opened.

Dana had expected to see the poor woman lying on the floor writhing in pain. But she saw no one. "Hello?" she called.

Another thud. This one coming from upstairs.

"Mrs. Randolph?" she called as she climbed the stairs. "Kitty?"

Still no answer.

At the top of the stairs she heard a sound coming from down the hall. A series of small thumps. One of the doors was partially open, the sound coming from inside.

She hurried down the hall, her mind racing as she shoved the door all the way open and stepped inside.

At once, she saw that the room was the master bedroom, large and plush, done in reds and golds.

At first she didn't see Kitty Randolph on the floor in front of the closet.

Dana realized why the woman hadn't heard her calling for her. Kitty Randolph was on her hands and knees, muttering to herself as she dug in the back of the huge closet. One shoe after another came flying out to land behind the woman.

Dana stumbled back, bumping into the door as one shoe almost hit her.

Kitty Randolph froze. Her frightened expression was chilling as she turned and saw Dana.

"I'm sorry if I frightened you," Dana said, afraid she would give the elderly woman a heart attack. "I rang the bell, then tried the door when I heard a sound…" She noticed the bruise on Kitty's cheek.

The older woman's hand went to it. "I am so clumsy." She looked from Dana to the floor covered with shoes.

Dana followed her gaze. The bedroom carpet was littered with every color and kind of shoe imaginable from shoes the judge had worn sole-bare to out-of-date sandals and pumps covered with dust.

"I was just cleaning out the closet," Kitty said awkwardly, trying to get to her feet. She had a shoe box clutched under one arm. "My husband was a pack rat. Saved everything. And I'm just as bad."

Dana reached a hand out to help her, but the older woman waved it away.

As Kitty rose, Dana saw the woman pick up a high-heeled shoe from the floor, looking at it as if surprised to see it.

She tossed it back into the closet and turned her attention to Dana. "I see you brought my fabric."

Dana had forgotten all about it. Embarrassed by frightening the woman, she thrust the bag at her.

Kitty took it, studying Dana as she put the shoe box she held onto the clean surface of the vanity. "How foolish of me to leave my package at your shop. You really shouldn't have gone out of your way to bring it to me."

"It was no trouble. I wanted to see you anyway to ask you if my sister stopped by to see you last night."

The older woman frowned. "What would give you that idea?"

"Nancy Harper said she saw Stacy drive down the road toward your house."

"That woman must have no time to do anything but look out the window," Kitty Randolph said irritably. "If your sister drove down here, I didn't see her." She turned to place the fabric package next to the shoe box on the vanity. She fiddled with the lid of the shoe box for a moment. "Why would Stacy come to see me?"

"I have no idea. I'd hoped you might." A lot of people drove cars like her sister's and it had been dark out. "Nancy Harper must have been mistaken," Dana said, glancing again at the shoes on the floor. "Can I help you with these?"

"No, you have better things to do, I'm sure," Kitty said as she stepped over the shoes and took Dana's arm, turning her toward the door. "Thank you again for bringing my fabric. You really shouldn't have."

It wasn't until Dana was driving away that she remembered the high heel Kitty Randolph had thrown back into the closet. She couldn't imagine the woman wearing anything with a heel that high. Or that color, either.

But then, who knew what Kitty Randolph had been like when she was young.

At the turn back onto Highway 191, Dana dialed her friend. "Hilde?"

"Is everything all right?"

"Fine. Listen, I was just thinking. I'm so close to Bozeman I thought I'd drive down and see my dad. I called and he's doing better. They said I could see him. Unless it's so busy there that you need me?"

"Go see your dad," Hilde said without hesitation. "I can handle things here. Anyway, it's slowed down this afternoon. I was thinking that if it doesn't pick up, I might close early."

"Do," Dana said. "We've made more than our quota for the month in the past few days."

"Tell your dad hello for me."

Dana hung up. She did want to see her father, but she also hoped that Stacy had been by to see him.

But when she reached the hospital, her father was still groggy, just as he'd been that morning. She didn't bring up anything that might upset him and only stayed for a few minutes as per the nurse's instructions.

As Dana was leaving, she stopped at the nurses' station to inquire about her father's visitors.

"Your brother was here," the nurse said. "That's the only visitor he's had today."

"My brother?"

"The skinny one."

Clay. That meant that neither Jordan nor Stacy had been here.

"But there have been a lot of calls checking on his condition," the nurse added.

Dana thanked her and headed back toward the ranch. She wanted to get a change of clothing if she was going to be staying at Hud's again tonight.

She knew she was being silly, wanting to slow things down. She loved Hud. He loved her. They'd spent too much time apart as it was. So why was she so afraid?

Because she didn't believe they could just pick up where they'd left off. They'd both changed. Didn't they need to get to know each other again—everything else that was going on aside?

And yet even as she thought it, she knew that the chemistry they shared was still there as well as the love. She knew what was holding her back. This investigation. Until Ginger Adams's killer was caught, Dana didn't feel safe. And she had no idea why.

As she drove down the road to the ranch house, she saw the tracks in the snow. Hud would have driven in to feed Joe. But there was at least another set of tire tracks. Someone else had been to the house today.

ZOEY SKINNER WAS FILLING salt and pepper shakers during the slow time between lunch and dinner in the large West Yellowstone café.

Hud couldn't say he remembered her. But she wasn't the kind of woman who stood out. Quite the opposite, she tended to blend into her surroundings.

The café was empty this time of the day, with it being a little too early yet for dinner.

He took a chair at a table in a far corner and glanced out the window at the walls of snow.

The town had changed over the years since the advent of snowmobiles. Where once winters were off season and most of the businesses closed and lay dormant under deep snowbanks, now the town literally buzzed with activity.

A large group of snowmobilers in their one-piece suits, heavy boots and dark-shielded helmets roared past in a cloud of blue smoke and noise.

"Coffee?"

He turned to find Zoey Skinner standing over his table, a menu tucked under her arm, a coffeepot in one hand and a cup in the other.

"Please. Cream and sugar."

Zoey was boney-thin, her arms corded from years of waiting tables, her legs webbed with blue veins although she was no more than in her early forties.

She filled the cup, produced both sugar and cream packages from her apron pocket. "Menu?"

He shook his head. "Just coffee, thanks. And if you have a moment—" he said, flashing his badge "—I'm Marshal Hudson Savage. I'd like to ask you a few questions."

She stared down at the badge, then slowly lifted her gaze to his. "This is about Ginger, isn't it?"

He nodded.

She dropped into the chair opposite his, her body suddenly limp as a rag doll's. She put the coffeepot on the table and cradled her head in her hands as she looked at him.

"I always wondered what happened to her," she said. "I heard that she'd been found in that well and I couldn't believe it."

"When was the last time you saw her?" he asked, taking out his notebook and pen.

"The night she left to get married."

"She was getting *married*?"

"Well, not right away." Zoey's face softened. "Ginger was so happy and excited."

"Who was she marrying?"

He saw her face close. "She said it was better I didn't know. Better that no one knew until they were married."

He studied the small, mousy-haired waitress. "Why was it so important to keep it a secret?"

"Ginger was afraid of jinxing it, you know? She'd been disappointed so many times before."

He didn't believe that for a minute. "Was it possible this man was married?" He saw the answer in Zoey's face. Bull's-eye. "So maybe that's why she didn't want anyone to know. Maybe he hadn't told his wife he was leaving her yet."

Zoey frowned and chewed at her lower lip. "Ginger just wanted to be loved. That's all. You know, have someone love her and take care of her." He got the feeling that Zoey not only knew who the man was but she also knew something else, something she wanted to tell him and for some reason was afraid to.

He took a shot in the dark. "This man, did he have money? He must have been older. Powerful?" The kind of man a woman like Ginger would have been attracted to.

Zoey looked away but not before he'd seen the answer in her eyes along with the fear. He felt his heart rate quicken. He was getting close. Was it possible the man was still around?

"Zoey, someone threw your best friend down a well, but when that didn't kill her, he shot her and left her there to die."

All the color drained from her face.

"Before she died, she tried to crawl out," he said.

A cry escaped Zoey's lips. She covered her mouth, her eyes wide and filled with tears.

"Ginger wanted desperately to live. Whoever threw her down that well was trying to get rid of her for good. If this man she was going to marry really loved her, then he would want you to tell me everything you know."

Zoey pulled a napkin from the container on the table and wiped at her eyes. "What about the baby?"

"Baby?"

Zoey nodded. "She was pregnant. Just a few weeks along."

That explained why there hadn't been another skeleton in the well.

Ginger hadn't been far enough along for there to be any evidence of a baby in a pile of bones at the bottom of a well.

But Hud realized it did give the father of the baby a motive for murder. "Did Ginger tell the father about the baby?" Zoey looked down. "Let me guess, he didn't want the baby."

"He *did*," Zoey protested, head coming up. "Ginger said he promised to take care of her and the baby."

"Maybe he did," Hud said solemnly. "Didn't you suspect something was wrong when you didn't hear from her again or she didn't come back for her things?"

"She took everything she wanted with her."

"Didn't she have a car?"

"She sold that."

"But didn't you think it was strange when you didn't hear from her?" he persisted.

"I just thought when things didn't work out that she was embarrassed, you know?"

He stared at Zoey, all his suspicions confirmed. "What made you think things didn't work out?"

She saw her mistake and tried to cover. "I never heard that she got married so…"

"You know things didn't work out because you knew who the man was. He's still in town, isn't he, Zoey? He never left his wife. He killed your friend and her baby and he got away with it."

Her face filled with alarm. "He wouldn't hurt her. He *loved* her." Her expression changed ever so slightly. She'd remembered something, something that made her doubt what she'd just said.

"They fought?" he guessed. "He ever hit her?" Hud was pretty sure he had, given what he suspected the man had done to Ginger at the end.

"Once. But that was just because he didn't want her wearing the engagement ring until…you know… until he was ready for them to announce it," she said. "Ginger forgot to take it off and was wearing the ring around town."

"Engagement ring?"

She nodded. "They fought about it. He wanted her to give it back so she didn't forget and wear it in public again. She refused. He hit her and tried to take it back."

Hud thought of the crime lab's report on the broken fingers of Ginger's left hand.

"What did this ring look like?" he asked, trying to keep the fear out of his voice.

"It was shaped like a diamond only it was green," she said. "He told Ginger it was an emerald, a really expensive one. It looked like it really was. And there were two diamonds, too. So don't you see? He wouldn't have given her an expensive ring like that unless he loved her, right?"

Chapter Thirteen

Dana pulled into the yard in front of the ranch house and parked, relieved to see no other vehicles. She'd worried she would come home to find Jordan searching the house again.

She wondered what he'd been up to all day since apparently he hadn't visited their father in the hospital. Why had Jordan lied about when he'd gotten into town if he hadn't been the one who'd put the doll in the well, who'd left the chocolates, who'd been trying to drive her from the ranch?

Getting out of the pickup, she walked to the porch. Someone had shoveled the steps. Hud no doubt.

Joe came around the side of the porch from his doghouse wagging his tail. He was pretty much deaf but he still seemed to know when she came home.

She rubbed his graying head and climbed the porch, digging for her keys she'd tossed in her purse after forgetting she was locking up the house now.

But as she shoved open the door and looked inside, she wondered why she'd bothered. Someone had ransacked the place.

She cursed and looked down at Joe. He seemed as perplexed as she was. Had he even barked at the intruder? She doubted it. She watched him as he followed her into the torn-up living room. He wasn't even sniffing around or acting as if a stranger had been here.

Because the person who'd torn up the house wasn't a stranger, she thought angrily. It was someone in her family, sure as hell. Jordan.

The house was a mess but nothing looked broken. It appeared he had done a frantic search not taking the time to put anything back where it had been.

She thought about calling Hud, but if she was right and Jordan had done this, his prints were already all over the house so it would prove nothing to find more of them.

Cursing under her breath, she took off her coat and went to work, putting the living room back in order. She had to pull out the vacuum since one of the plants had been turned over and there was dirt everywhere.

She promised she would fix whoever had done this as she turned on the vacuum. Over the roar of the vacuum, she didn't hear the car drive up, didn't hear someone come up the steps and tap at the door. Nor did she see her visitor peer inside to see if she was alone.

HUD DIALED NEEDLES AND PINS the minute he left the Lonesome Pine Café and Zoey.

"Hilde, I need to speak to Dana."

"Hud? Is everything all right?"

"No," he said. "Tell me she's still there."

He heard Hilde sigh and his heart dropped like a stone.

"Hud, she left earlier. She ran an errand and then went to visit her dad. But she should be at the ranch by now."

Hud groaned. Of course she would want to visit her dad again. He should have put a deputy on her. Right. Wouldn't Dana have loved having Norm Turner following her around all day? But Hud would have gladly put up with her wrath just to know she was safe right now.

"Hud, what is it?" Hilde cried. "Do you want me to try to find her?"

"No, I'm not that far away. I can get there quicker." He disconnected, his mind racing with everything he'd learned. The highway was slick with ice. He drove as fast as he could, dialing the ranch house as he did.

The phone rang and rang. Either Dana wasn't home yet or— The woman didn't even have an answering machine?

His radio squawked. He closed the cell phone and grabbed the radio. "Marshal Savage."

"It's Deputy Stone," Liza said, all business. "Angus Cardwell's .38. It doesn't match. Not even close. It wasn't the murder weapon." She sounded disappointed since she'd been so sure it was—based on Angus Cardwell's reaction to her finding the gun in his pickup.

He took in the information, his heart racing a little faster. He'd been sure it would be the gun. And after what Dana had told him about Angus's argument and heart attack, Hud had suspected Jordan Cardwell would turn out to be the person who'd used the gun. Could he be wrong about Jordan's involvement?

"But we do have a match on the prints found on both the doll and the box of chocolates," she said. "They were Jordan Cardwell's."

Jordan. He'd suspected Jordan of a lot more. What bothered Hud was the incident with the doll in the well and the box of undoctored chocolates didn't go together. One was so innocuous. The other was possibly attempted murder on Dana. At the very least, assault on an officer of the law.

"I'm on my way back from Missoula," Liza said. "Anything else you want me to do?"

"No, it's supposed to be your day off. Drive carefully." He disconnected and radioed his other deputy.

"Deputy Turner," Norm said.

"Pick up Jordan Cardwell ASAP," Hud ordered. He heard the deputy's feet hit the floor.

"On what charge, sir?"

"Let's start with assault on a marshal," Hud said. Jordan's mother and Kitty Randolph had been friends. Jordan could have had access to Kitty's ring. "Just find him and get him locked up. Let me know the minute he's behind bars."

As he disconnected, Hud thought about Kitty Randolph's emerald ring. He now knew how it had ended up with Ginger Adams in the well. He just hoped to hell he was wrong about who had killed her.

As DANA SHUT OFF THE VACUUM, she sensed someone watching her and turned, startled to see a shadow cross the porch.

The doorbell rang. She opened the door and blinked in surprise. "Mrs. Randolph?" The bruise on the older woman's face was darker than it had been earlier in the day. She had what appeared to be that same shoe box under one arm and her hat was askew.

Kitty Randolph smiled. "Hello, dear. I'm sorry to drop by unannounced like this." She looked past Dana. "Did I catch you at a bad time? I was hoping to talk to you. Alone, if possible?"

"Of course, come in."

"You're sure it's not a bad time?" Kitty asked, her gaze going again past Dana into the house.

"Not at all. I was just doing some cleaning myself."

The older woman turned and stuck out one leg to show off her blue slacks. "That thread you sold me was the perfect color blue, don't you think?"

Dana admired the recently hemmed slacks, telling herself this couldn't possibly be the reason Kitty had driven all the way out here. It was probably the upcoming fundraiser. Dana groaned at the thought. The fundraiser was weeks away. Was she going to find Kitty on her doorstep every day until it was over?

"Can I take your coat?" Dana asked, wondering what was in the worn-looking shoe box. Probably old apron patterns. Or recipes.

"The judge always liked me in blue," Kitty said as if she hadn't heard Dana. "That was until his tastes changed to red."

Dana smiled, remembering the red-and-gold master bedroom—and the bright red high-heeled shoe Kitty had tossed back into the closet earlier at her house.

"Would you like something to drink?" Dana asked. "I could put on some coffee. Or would you prefer tea?" She hoped Hud showed up soon, as he'd promised earlier. He might be the only way she could get rid of the woman.

"Neither, thank you. I couldn't help thinking about your visit to my house today," she said, glancing toward the kitchen again. "Sometimes I am so forgetful. You did say you're alone, didn't you?"

"Yes." Was it possible Kitty Randolph had forgotten that Stacy had visited her last night? "Did you remember something about Stacy?"

"Stacy, interesting woman." Her twinkling blue eyes settled on Dana's face. "How could two sisters be so different? You're so much like your mother and your sister is…" She raised a disapproving brow. "She's an alley cat like your father. But then some women are born to it."

Dana frowned and almost found herself defending her sister. Instead she studied the older woman, noticing that Kitty seemed…different somehow. Oddly animated. She'd always been a soft-spoken, refined woman who'd obviously come from old wealth. She'd never heard Kitty talk like this.

"This must all be very upsetting for you," Dana said. Ginger Adams's body being found in the well had dredged up the judge's murder. Of course Kitty would be distraught.

"Yes, dear, I can't tell you how upsetting it's been." Kitty stepped over to one of the old photographs on the wall and Dana noticed with a start that it was of the old homestead up on the hillside.

"Did I ever tell you that the judge's family were well drillers?" Kitty asked.

"I didn't know that."

Kitty turned and smiled. "The judge's father drilled most every well around here. Including the one up at your family's old homestead."

THE RADIO SQUAWKED AS HUD neared Big Sky—and the Cardwell Ranch.

"I've got Jordan Cardwell here, sir," Deputy Norm Turner said. "He insists on talking to you for his one phone call."

Hud breathed a sigh of relief that Jordan was behind bars. Now at least Dana should be safe. "Put him on."

"Is this about the other night, that thing with the doll and the well?" Jordan demanded.

"You mean, where you tried to kill me?" Hud said.

"I'm telling you the same thing I told Dana, I had nothing to do with it."

"You lied about when you flew in, you lied about your relationship with Ginger Adams, and you expect me to believe you? Save your breath, your fingerprints were found on both the doll—and the box of chocolates."

"I did fly in the day before, the instant I heard about the bones in the well, and I knew Ginger," Jordan said. "I probably touched the stupid doll when I was searching for the will. And I also gave Dana the chocolates. I wanted her to think they were from you. I thought it might make her treat you a little nicer and that it would speed up the investigation so we could get on with selling the ranch."

"You are so thoughtful."

"Listen to me, I do care about my sister," Jordan said. "If I didn't put some stupid doll down in the well to scare Dana, then who did? That person doesn't seem to be behind bars in your quaint little jail."

Hud was silent for a moment, thinking this might be the first time he'd ever believed anything that had come out of Jordan Cardwell's mouth. "Did you steal a ring and give it to Ginger Adams?"

"What? Look, Ginger and I didn't last a month. As soon as she found out I didn't have any money…"

Hud pulled the list of registered .38-caliber gun owners out of his pocket as he drove. It was starting to get dark in the canyon. He had to turn on the overhead light in the SUV, taking his attention off the road in short glances as he scanned the list again.

He found the name he'd feared would be on the sheet. He hadn't even thought to look for it before.

Probably because it never dawned on him to look for Judge Raymond Randolph's name. What were the chances he would have been killed with his own gun? The same gun that had killed Ginger Adams?

Hud threw down the sheet, snapped off the light and said, "Let me talk to the deputy." He told Norm to keep Jordan locked up and to get over to Kitty Randolph's and make sure she didn't go anywhere.

Then Hud tried Dana's number again, driving as fast as possible. He had to get to Dana. Every instinct told him she was in trouble.

DANA FELT A SENSE OF DISQUIET settle over her as she stared at Kitty Randolph. "The judge's father drilled the homestead well?"

The phone rang.

"The judge knew every well his father had drilled," Kitty said proudly. "He took me to most of them when we were dating. Most women wouldn't think that very romantic nowadays. But the judge never wanted to forget where he came from. Common well drillers. But that was one reason he was so cheap. The judge was the only one in his family to go to college, you know."

The phone rang again. Mind racing, Dana barely heard it as she watched Kitty move around the room, picking up knickknacks, touching old photographs, admiring antiques that had belonged to Dana's mother's family. The older woman still had the shoe box tucked under her arm.

"Your mother, now there was a woman," Kitty said as she circled the room. "I admired her so much. Your father put her through so much and yet she never complained. She proved she could make it without him just fine. I wish I had been more like her."

Another ring. "I need to get that," Dana said, but for some reason didn't want to leave Kitty alone.

"Have I told you how much you look like your mother?"

"Yes, you've mentioned it," Dana said, thinking again about what Kitty had said about the judge's family drilling the old homestead well.

"It's funny, for a moment earlier today when I saw you standing behind me at my house, I thought you were your mother," Kitty said, then gave her head a light shake. "Sometimes I am so foolish. Your mother was such a strong woman. I admired the way she took care of *her* problems."

Dana felt a chill crawl up her spine as she recalled a comment Jordan had made about how their mother had been capable of killing Ginger Adams and dumping her down the old well.

"Is there something you wanted to tell me about my mother?" Dana asked, frightened of the answer and suddenly afraid of what was in that shoe box under the older woman's arm.

"Oh, Dana, don't be coy with me," Kitty said, her smile shifting ever so slightly. "I know you saw the shoe."

The shoe? The phone rang again. She realized it might be Hud. He'd be worried if she didn't answer it.

"I don't know what shoe you're talking about." Dana had seen a lot of shoes on the floor of Kitty's bedroom and the older woman digging in the closet as if looking for more. She wondered if the older woman wasn't getting senile as she glanced at the shoe box still curled in the crook of the woman's arm.

"The red high heel, dear, you know the one," Kitty said. "Oh, didn't your boyfriend tell you? Only one was found in the well. The other one was in the judge's closet. I'd forgotten all about it until my dear friend Rupert Milligan happened to mention that one red high heel had been found in the well. Rupert has a little crush on me." She actually blushed.

Dana felt her heart stop cold at the realization of what Kitty was saying.

The phone, she really needed to answer the phone. She started to move toward the kitchen.

"Let it ring, dear," Kitty said, and opened the shoe box.

Dana stared in shock as Kitty brought out a .38 and pointed it at her. Dana glanced toward the front door where her shotgun was leaning against the wall as the phone continued to ring.

"I wouldn't if I were you, dear," Kitty said, leveling the gun at Dana's heart. "Let's take a walk."

The phone stopped ringing. "A walk?" Dana said into the deathly silence that followed. What if Hud had been calling to say he was running late? "Mrs. Randolph—"

"Kitty. Call me Kitty, dear." The hand holding the gun was steady, the glint in the twinkling blue eyes steely. "Get your coat. It's cold out."

"I don't understand," Dana said as she carefully took her coat from the hook, afraid she understood only too well. The shotgun was within reach but it wasn't loaded. Even if it had been, she suspected she would never be able to fire it before Kitty Randolph pulled the trigger.

"I'll explain it to you on our walk," Kitty said agreeably as she jabbed the gun into Dana's back. "We really need to get moving, though. It gets darks so early in the canyon, especially this time of year. We wouldn't want to step in a hole, now would we?" She laughed as Dana opened the door and they descended the porch steps.

Dana suspected she knew where they were headed long before Kitty motioned her up the road toward the old homestead—and the well.

"Oh, and in case you're wondering, the judge taught me how to use a gun," Kitty said. "I'm sure he regretted it since I was a much better shot than he was."

As they walked up the road, Dana saw that a vehicle had been up the hill recently. The same person who'd ransacked the house? Her mind raced. Was it possible Jordan was up here planning to pull another stunt to scare her into selling the ranch?

She couldn't believe it had been Jordan—didn't want to believe it. But right now, she would love to see any member of her family.

"Ginger was a tramp, you know," Kitty said as they walked up the road. The older woman was surprisingly spry for her age. "Your mother wasn't the least bit fazed by her. She knew your father would never have left her for a woman like Ginger Adams. For all your father's flaws, he had better taste than that."

Dana wouldn't have bet on that, she thought as she looked up at the homestead chimney. Had she seen movement up there? Twilight had turned the sky gray.

From the highway she could hear the hum of tires. Hud was on his way. He'd said he would meet her at the ranch house before she got off work. Except she'd come home early. Still he should be here soon. Unless he really had been calling to say he was running late.

"The judge, the old fool, thought he was in love with Ginger," Kitty was saying. "He thought I would give him a divorce so he could marry her. He forgot that the money was all mine. But even then, he would have left me for her and lived on nothing, he was that besotted with her. After thirty years of marriage. Can you imagine? She was just a *child*."

Dana heard the pain in the older woman's voice and looked up, surprised they had reached the old homestead in record time. No wonder, with Kitty nudging her along with the gun.

"He begged me to let him go, the stupid old fool. But I had insurance, something I knew he'd done that could get him disbarred, disgraced and leave him penniless so he wouldn't be able to support his precious Ginger and their baby." Kitty sounded as if she was crying. "We couldn't have a child, you know. But this tramp... I remember the night he brought me that red high-heeled shoe. He was sobbing like a baby. 'Look what you made me do,' he kept saying. 'Oh, God, look what you've made me do.' As if he didn't have a choice."

Dana stumbled and turned to look at Kitty, shocked by the revelation. The judge had killed Ginger Adams on his wife's orders?

"Oh, don't look so shocked," Kitty Randolph said. "Imagine what I would have done that night if I'd known he'd given her my ring? It was the only decent piece of jewelry he'd ever bought me. It never meant that much to me because I'd had to force him to buy it for our anniversary. But even if I never wore it, it was mine and he gave it to that woman. And then to hear it turned up in your well—with *her*."

Dana was too stunned to speak for a moment.

"Let's get this over with," Kitty said and jabbed Dana with the gun, prodding her toward the well opening. Kitty's voice changed, sounding almost childlike. "You don't want to get too close to the edge of the well, dear. You might fall in. It's only natural that you would be curious. Or perhaps you're distraught over the news about your mother. Sorry, dear, but after you're gone it's going to come out that your mother killed Ginger. Mary wouldn't mind, after all she's dead."

Dana balked. "You wouldn't blame my mother."

"I've given it a lot of thought," Kitty said matter-of-factly. "Your mother was afraid, living out here alone, and I lent her the judge's .38. I'd completely forgotten the gun was in the closet until the marshal called to say that Ginger had been killed with the same gun the judge was."

"No one will believe my mother killed Ginger Adams—*and* your husband."

"You are so right, dear. Your sister, the common thief, took the gun while it was in your mother's possession and killed the judge. I'll work out the details later. But when it comes out about your sister stealing fundraiser money and me having it all on video…"

"*You're* the one who forced Stacy to make it look like she and Hud had slept together."

"Oh, dear, you are so smart," Kitty said as she backed Dana toward the well. "I was quite the mastermind if I say so myself. First I hired the Kirk brothers to mow my lawn and then I planted the judge's cuff links and pocket watch in their car. I said I'd be at my sister's that night. With cell phones, no one can tell where you are. Aren't they amazing devices?"

As Kitty backed her into the darkness, Dana could feel the well coming up behind her.

"The judge was at his stupid Toastmasters. I called and told him I thought I'd left the stove on, then I waited until he was on his way home before I called those awful Kirk brothers and told them I'd left them a bonus and to stop by the house and pick it up. The door was open. It was all too easy. You should have seen the judge's face when I shot him twice in the chest."

Dana grimaced. If she'd had any doubt that Kitty would shoot her, she didn't now.

"The Kirk brothers arrived right after that," she continued. "They reacted just as I knew they would when they heard the sirens. Hud's father had been trying to get the goods on them for years. I knew he'd chase them to the ends of the earth. And he literally did. All I had to do was make it look as if the Kirks had broken into my house and then go to my sister's and wait for the terrible news."

Dana stopped moving. She could feel the well directly behind her. One more step and she would fall into it. "Why set up Hud with my sister?"

"Stacy had to do whatever I told her and I knew how badly Hud's father wanted to put those awful Kirk brothers away. He was more apt to believe they had robbed my house and killed my husband than your boyfriend." Kitty smiled, pleased with herself. "Anyway, by doing that I freed you up for my nephew."

"Your *nephew?*"

Something moved by the chimney and Dana watched as a large dark figure came out of the shadows behind Kitty. Jordan. Let it be Jordan.

"Step back, dear," Kitty said. "Let's not make this any more painful than we have to."

As the figure grew closer, Dana saw the man's face. Not Jordan. "Lanny, be careful, she has a gun!"

Kitty began to laugh, but didn't turn as if she thought Dana was kidding. Then Dana watched in horror as Lanny made no attempt to disarm Kitty.

He leaned down to plant a kiss on the older woman's cheek. "Why would I hurt my dear auntie? Really, Dana, I can attest to how irrational you've been the last few days."

"Kitty is your aunt?"

"By marriage twice removed, but Dana you know that half the people in the canyon are related in some way, you shouldn't be surprised," Lanny said.

"Say your goodbyes, Lanny," Kitty said.

"You aren't going to let her do this," Dana said. "You and I were friends."

Lanny laughed. "Friends? But you are right about one thing, I'm not going to let her do it. I'm going to take care of you, Dana, because quite frankly I'd rather see you dead than with Hudson Savage."

He reached for her and in the twilight she saw the hard glint of anger in his eyes—the same look she'd seen at the restaurant the night of her birthday.

She dodged his grasp and felt one of the stones around the well bump against her ankle as she was forced back. She looked over her shoulder, estimating whether or not she could jump the opening. Maybe if she had a run at it, but the hole was too wide, the snow too slick around it.

She put out her hands, bracing her feet, ready to take Lanny down into the well with her if he grabbed for her again.

"You can make this easy on yourself, Dana. Or fight right up until the end." Lanny smiled. "Makes no difference to me."

"But it does to me," Hud said from out of the darkness.

Both Lanny and his aunt turned in surprise. Dana saw her chance. She dove at Lanny, slamming her palms into his chest with all of her strength. He stumbled backward, colliding with his aunt Kitty, but managed to grasp Dana's sleeve and pull her down, as well.

The air exploded with a gunshot and Dana couldn't be sure who'd fired it as she fell to the ground next to Lanny.

She scrambled away from him but he grabbed her ankle and crawled, dragging her, toward the well opening. She noticed that his side bloomed dark red and she realized he'd been shot. But his grip on her ankle was strong.

She tried to latch on to anything she could reach but there was nothing to hang on to and the snow was slick and she slid across it with little effort on Lanny's part.

More gunshots and Dana saw now that Kitty was firing wildly into the darkness. Dana couldn't see Hud, wasn't even sure now that she'd heard his voice. Lanny had a death grip on her leg.

The black gaping hole of the well was so close now that she felt the cold coming up from the bottom.

This time the gunshots were louder, echoing across the hillside. Dana saw Kitty stumble, heard her cry. Out of the corner of her eye, Dana watched Kitty start to fall.

Dana kicked out at Lanny with her free leg. His grip on her ankle loosened as his aunt tripped over him, but managed to remain standing.

He let go of Dana's ankle and for an instant they were all frozen in time. Kitty was looking down at her blue slacks. One leg appeared black in the darkening light. Dana scooted out of Lanny's grasp and was getting to her feet when she heard Hud order, "Put down the gun, Mrs. Randolph."

Kitty looked up, her spine straightening, her chin going up. "I had a bad feeling when you came back to town, Hudson Savage." She smiled and Dana watched the rest play out in slow, sick motion.

Kitty dropped the gun, but Lanny grabbed it up and started to turn it on Dana. She saw the crazed look in his eyes as he gripped the gun and frantically felt for the trigger.

Hud's weapon made a huge booming sound in the deafening silence. The shot caught Lanny in the chest but he was still trying to pull the trigger as another shot exploded and he fell back, his head lolling to one side on the edge of the well.

Dana wrenched the gun from his hands and crawled back away from him and the well.

Kitty was still standing there, head up. The one leg of her slacks looked black with blood. She didn't seem to notice Lanny lying on the ground next to her.

Dana turned as Hud came out of the shadows, his weapon still pointed at Kitty. Out of the corner of her eye, she caught the movement and heard Hud yell, "No!"

Dana turned in time to see Kitty Randolph smile as she stepped back and dropped into the well.

A few seconds later Dana heard the sickening thud as Kitty hit the bottom. But by then, Hud was pulling Dana into his arms and telling her he loved her, over and over again. In the distance she could hear the wail of sirens.

Chapter Fourteen

Hud parked by the Hebgen Lake house and got out, noting that his father's vehicle was in the garage and there were no fresh tracks.

But when he knocked at the door, he got no answer. He tried the knob, not surprised when the door opened in. "Dad?" he called. The word sounded funny and he tried to remember the last time he'd said it.

As he moved through the house, it became more apparent that Brick wasn't there. Hud felt his pulse start as he reminded himself how old his father had seemed the other day, then recalled with shame and embarrassment what he'd said to Brick.

But Hud knew the panicky feeling in the pit of his stomach had more to do with what he hadn't yet said to his father.

"Dad?" he called again.

No answer. He glanced into the bedrooms. Both empty, beds made. Hud had never expected his father to keep such a neat house. Hud's mother had hated housework.

The kitchen was also empty, still smelling faintly of bacon and coffee. But as he looked out the window across the frozen white expanse of the lake, he spotted a lone figure squatting on the ice.

Hud opened the back door and followed the well-worn footprints across patches of glistening wind-crusted ice and drifted snow, his boot soles making a crunching sound as he walked toward his father.

Dressed in a heavy coat and hat, Brick Savage sat on a log stump, a short ice-fishing pole in his gloved hands. The fishing line disappeared down into the perfect hole cut in the ice at his feet.

His father looked up and smiled. "Heard the news. You solved both murders. Figured you would."

Just then the rod jerked. Brick set the hook and hauled a large rainbow trout out of the slushy water and up onto the ice. He picked up the flopping trout, unhooked it and dropped it back into the water.

Hud stood, trying to put into words everything he wanted—needed—to say to his father. Hud had been so sure that his father had set him up so he could kill Judge Raymond Randolph and frame the Kirk brothers. "Dad, I—"

"There's an extra rod," Brick said, cutting him off. He motioned to the rod resting against an adjacent stump.

"You knew I'd be showing up?" Hud asked in surprise.

His dad smiled. "I'd hoped you would."

"There's some things I need to say to you."

Brick shook his head. "Your coming here today says everything I need to hear." He reached over and picked up the short rod and handed it to his son. "If you want, we could keep a few fish and cook them up for lunch. Or if you're in a hurry—"

"No hurry. I haven't had trout in a long time," Hud said, taking a seat across from his father. "I could stay to eat trout for lunch."

His dad nodded and Hud thought he glimpsed something he'd never seen, tears in his father's eyes. Brick dropped his head to bait his hook and when he looked up again, the tears were gone. If they were ever there.

He watched his father, thinking he might call Dana after lunch to see if she'd like trout for dinner tonight. "I've been offered the marshal job," he said as he baited his line and dropped it into the hole.

"I'm not surprised."

"I heard you put in a good word for me," Hud said, feeling his throat tighten.

"Rupert's got a big mouth," Brick said but smiled. "The canyon's lucky to get you. Dana pleased about it?"

He nodded and hooked into a fish. "You know about Rupert and Kitty Randolph?"

"I knew he liked her. He's taking it all pretty hard. He likes to think he's smarter than most people when it comes to figuring out criminals," Brick said.

"Kitty fooled a lot of people."

"Yes, she did," Brick said.

They spent the rest of the morning fishing, talking little. Later while Brick was frying up the trout for lunch, Hud called Dana and told her he was bringing trout for dinner.

"You ask her to marry you yet?" Brick asked after he hung up and they were sitting down to eat lunch.

"I'm going to tonight," Hud said.

Without a word, his dad got up from the table and returned a few minutes later with a small velvet box. He set it beside Hud's plate and sat. "I know you bought her an engagement ring before. I couldn't afford an engagement ring for your mother so she never had one. But I was wondering if you'd like to have your grandmother's?"

Hud frowned. He'd never known either of his grandparents. His father's parents were dead before he was born and from what he'd heard, his mother's family had disowned his mother when she'd married Brick. "My grandmother...?"

"Christensen. Your grandmother on your mother's side," he said, and handed the small velvet box to Hud. "She left it to me in her will. I guess it was her way of saying she was sorry for making it so hard on your mother for marrying me." He shrugged. "Anyway, I know your mother would want you to have it."

Hud opened the small velvet box and pulled back in surprise. "It's beautiful."

Brick helped himself to the trout. "Just like Dana."

Hud studied his father. "Thank you."

"There's some money, too," Brick said. "Probably not near enough to pay off Dana's brothers and sister and keep the ranch, though."

"I doubt there is enough money in the world for that," Hud said. "Jordan won't be happy until the ranch is sold, but I'm sure he'll be disappointed when he realizes how small his share is. He would have been much better off if his mother's new will had been found. He would have gotten money for years from the ranch instead of a lump sum, and in the end come out way ahead."

"But he wants it all now," Brick said. "You think he found the new will and destroyed it?"

"Probably."

Brick handed him the plate of trout.

"I got a call from Stacy Cardwell this morning. She's in Las Vegas. She said Kitty threatened to kill her when she stopped by the woman's place the night before she left. I guess Stacy thought she could get some traveling money out of Kitty as if blackmail went both ways," Hud said, shaking his head.

"It's a wonder Kitty didn't shoot her on the spot."

Hud remembered Dana's story about finding Kitty on her hands and knees digging in the closet. "Probably would have but she'd forgotten she still had the .38. There was a struggle, though. Dana said Kitty had a bruise on her cheek."

Brick nodded. "You could bring Stacy back to face charges."

Hud shook his head. Both Lanny and Kitty were dead. It was over.

He and Brick ate in silence for a while, and then Hud said, "I saw you with Ginger that night."

His father paused, then took a bite of fish. "I remembered after you were gone. I pulled her over that night. She'd been drinking. I thought about taking her in, made her get out of the car and go through the sobriety tests."

Hud recalled the sound of Ginger's laughter. As Hud had driven past, she'd been flirting with Brick, spinning around in that red dress and those bright red high-heeled shoes.

"I saw all her stuff in the back of her car," Brick said.

Hud wondered if the judge or Kitty had gotten rid of Ginger's belongings and her car. No one would have ever known about her death, if Warren hadn't seen her skull at the bottom of the Cardwell Ranch well.

"She told me she was leaving town," Brick was saying. "I told her to be careful. If I'd locked her up that night, she might still be alive."

DANA STOOD IN THE KITCHEN after Hud's call, looking up the hillside. There was no old chimney or foundation anymore. It was as if there'd never been an old homestead up there. Or an old well. A backhoe operator had filled in the well. Soon after the land was cleared, it had begun to snow again, covering up the scarred earth.

Dana thought she could get used to the new view, but it would take time. She frowned at the thought, realizing she didn't have time. After everything that had happened, she had given up her fight to save the ranch. Jordan was right. All she was doing was costing them all attorneys' fees and eventually, she would lose and have to sell anyway. She'd told Jordan he could list the property with a Realtor.

She turned away from the window, turning her thoughts, as well, to more pleasant things. Hud. She smiled, just thinking about him. They'd been inseparable, making love, talking about the future. Even now she missed him and couldn't wait for him to get back.

He was bringing trout for dinner. She was glad he'd gone up to see his father. Her mother had been right about one thing. Family. It *did* matter. Her own father was out of the hospital and planning to be back playing with Uncle Harlan in the band. They'd both offered to play at the wedding. Her father had promised to cut back on his drinking but Dana wasn't holding her breath. She was just glad to still have him.

She smiled, thinking of the wedding she and Hud would have. That is, if he asked her to marry him again.

Since Kitty Randolph's death, a lot of things had come out about the judge. Some of the things Hud had blamed on his father had been the judge's doing.

Hud had even realized that his mother's bitterness toward Brick was fueled by her family and that it had made Brick into the hard man he was when Hud was growing up.

The past few days had changed them all. At least Dana had decided she was ready to let go of all the old hurts and move on, whatever the future held.

She stopped in the middle of the kitchen as if she'd just felt a warm hand on her shoulder and it was as if she could feel her mother's presence. Wasn't this what her mother had wanted? For her to forgive and forget?

Dana smiled, the feeling warming her as she moved to the cupboard that held all her mother's cookbooks. Like her mother, she loved cookbooks, especially the old ones.

She pulled out her mother's favorite and ran her fingers over the worn cover. Maybe she would make Hud's favorite double-chocolate brownies from her mother's old recipe. She hadn't made them since Hud had left five years before.

As she opened the book, several sheets of lined paper fluttered to the floor. Stooping to pick them up, she caught sight of her mother's handwriting. Her heart leaped to her throat. Hurriedly, she unfolded the pages.

Her heart began to pound harder as she stared down at her mother's missing will.

* * * * *

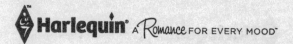

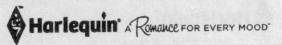

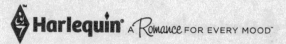

INSPIRATIONAL

Wholesome romances that touch the heart and soul.

Love Inspired®
Contemporary inspirational romances with Christian characters facing the challenges of life and love in today's world.

Love Inspired® Suspense
Heart-pounding tales of suspense, romance, hope and faith.

Love Inspired® Historical
Travel back in time and experience powerful and engaging stories of romance, adventure and faith.

Look for these and many other Love Inspired books wherever books are sold, including most bookstores, supermarkets, drugstores and discount stores.

INSPCAT2

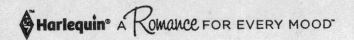

Choose a romance just for you
with
$1.⁰⁰ OFF
any Harlequin novel.

RECEIVE $1.00 OFF
any Harlequin novel.

Available wherever books are sold, including most bookstores, supermarkets, drugstores and discount stores.

Coupon expires January 31, 2012. Redeemable at participating retail outlets in the U.S. only. Limit one coupon per customer. Valid at participating retail outlets.

U.S. RETAILERS: Harlequin Enterprises Limited will pay the face value of this coupon plus 8¢ if submitted by customer for this specified product only. Any other use constitutes fraud. Coupon is nonassignable. Void if taxed, prohibited or restricted by law. Consumer must pay any government taxes. Void if copied. For reimbursement, submit coupons and proof of sales directly to: Harlequin Enterprises Limited, P.O. Box 880478, El Paso, TX 88588-0478, U.S.A. Cash value 1/100 cents. Limit one coupon per purchase. Valid in the U.S. only.

5 65373 00076 2   (8100)0 11766

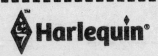